KILL COUNT

A TEAM REAPER THRILLER

MARK ALLEN

BRENT TOWNS

WOLFPACK PUBLISHING
— EST 2013 —

Kill Count
A Team Reaper novel
By Mark Allen

Based on Characters Created by Brent Towns
All rights reserved.

Published in the United States by Wolfpack Publishing, Las Vegas.

Wolfpack Publishing
6032 Wheat Penny Avenue
Las Vegas, NV 89122

wolfpackpublishing.com

Ebook ISBN 978-1-64119-621-5
Paperback ISBN 978-1-64119-622-2

KILL COUNT

CHAPTER 1

Lebron's Bar & Grill
New York City

As soon as the three men entered the bar, John 'Reaper' Kane knew they were going to be trouble. It might have had something to do with the skeleton masks covering their faces, but was more than likely the stubby Micro-Uzis they whipped out from beneath their long, loose-fitting coats. They sported a pair of the submachine guns, one in each hand. A piss-poor tactic for precision shooting, but perfect for saturating a room with bullets.

"Down!" Kane yelled, his right hand reaching under his jacket for the Sig-Sauer M17 semi-automatic holstered on his hip. With his left hand, he grabbed the edge of the heavy wooden table and with a grunt, flipped it over, sending beer bottles, silverware, and napkins flying everywhere. Right now, making a mess was the least of his concerns. The solid oak table was at least three inches thick, more than capable of stopping the 9mm rounds that were about to blister it.

The wood wouldn't hold forever, but hopefully long enough for the team to return fire and take out the hitters.

His teammates—Thurston and Traynor—reacted instantly to the threat, dropping down behind the overturned table and drawing their own Sigs. Mike Reardon—the DEA agent who had called this meeting—also drew his Glock 22 sidearm as he crouched down to avoid the imminent fusillade.

A woman screamed.

Swiveling his head to the left, Kane saw Reardon's wife Becky framed in the bathroom doorway, eyes wide as she saw the automatic weapons pointed at them.

"Becky!" Mike yelled. He started to rise to his feet, but Traynor pulled him down.

With no regard for his own skin, Kane threw himself into a sideways leap that he hoped would put his body in front of Becky. He fired a round in midair, the gun bucking in his fist. Not that he expected to hit anything—that kind of acrobatic marksmanship only worked in the movies—but he hoped to make the three gunmen hesitate.

It didn't work. As he hit the floor at Becky's feet, the Micro-Uzis cut loose with their distinctive full-auto staccato. Skidding to a stop against a barstool, he got his sights on the nearest gunman and drilled a double-tap into his face. The skeleton mask collapsed as the target's head snapped back in a spray of blood.

Adrenalin pulsed through Kane's system. Somewhere in the back of his mind, he realized that Becky had stopped screaming. The rest of the patrons had taken her place, crying out in pain and terror as auto-fire chopped them down, tearing through flesh and guts to rip the life right out of them.

In the blink of an eye, the bar became a kill-zone...

Twenty minutes earlier...

Another day, another backstreet bar. The thought put an amused smirk on Kane's face as he walked down a New York City street that wasn't the worst the Big Apple had to offer but was definitely a block or two off Broadway. There were no glitzy, neon-lit tourist traps beckoning down this street, though some instinct warned him there could be traps of a deadlier kind. This was a street of sinners, not saints. Who knew what danger lurked amidst the winos and whores?

Then again, he always felt that way lately—a constant tingle at the base of his neck, as if expecting a bullet. Too many days on the killing fields maybe. When you lived by the gun, sometimes it felt like you were forever in the crosshairs. He shrugged off the feeling, wondering why their contact had insisted on meeting so far off the grid.

He was accompanied by General Mary Thurston, the overseer of Team Reaper, the one who ultimately called the shots. She greenlit the jobs, and without her blessing, there was no mission.

To Kane's right was Pete Traynor. The former DEA undercover operative strolled along like he didn't have a care in the world, as if they were taking a nighttime walk down a Cancun beach instead of a seedy side-street.

Kane treated himself to a quick glance at Thurston. If she noticed him looking, she gave no indication, keeping her gaze straight ahead as they headed up the block to their meeting place. With her athletic build and long dark hair pulled back into a ponytail, she was definitely easy on the eyes, but Kane wasn't really interested. Not only was

Thurston the boss, but he and Cara had just recently ended things. He wasn't ready for another woman in his life.

As if reading his mind, Traynor asked, "Talked to Billings lately?"

Kane looked over at the ex-DEA agent. With his linebacker shoulders and rugged, mountain man beard, Traynor wasn't nearly as enjoyable to look at as Thurston. "Sure," Kane replied. "I talk to her all the time. She's a teammate."

Traynor grinned. "Not what I meant, Reaper, and you know it."

"What I know is that you can change the damn subject and tell me about this friend of yours we're meeting."

"Mike? The guy's one of the best undercover agents I ever worked with. Not sure there's a corner of Mexico he didn't run an op in."

"Riding a desk now, right?"

Traynor nodded. "Even the best can't stay under forever. He got burned, and they managed to pull him out just a half-step ahead of a cartel *sicario*. Then they put him behind a desk here on the east coast overseeing undercover ops."

"What's up with meeting in some shithole bar? Hasn't your buddy ever heard of an encrypted phone?"

Thurston said, "Cut him some slack, Kane. They kidnapped his son. He doesn't know who he can trust right now, so you can't blame him for being skittish."

Traynor slapped him on the shoulder with a hand big enough to palm a cinder block. "Look on the bright side. Meeting in a bar gives you an excuse to have a beer."

Kane pointedly looked at the dingy surroundings. "Wherever we're going, I'm betting they only serve rotgut."

Traynor shook his head. "Nah, I doubt there'll be any Coors Light at this place."

Two blocks later, "this place" turned out to be a small but cleaner-than-expected establishment simply called Lebron's Bar & Grill. Neon beer signs glowed in the front window. It was basically just one long rectangular room with a mahogany-and-brass bar running down the right side and two rows of wooden tables on the left. There was no dancefloor as this was clearly the kind of place you came to drink, not bust a move. A jukebox squatted against the back wall next to the unisex bathroom, playing an old hair-metal ballad. Something about flying to the angels.

The clientele ran counter to Kane's expectations. No dirtbags or deviants, just seemingly normal people scattered about, mostly solo, with a few couples mixed in. Down at the far end of the bar, a well-groomed black bartender mixed a Jack and Coke for an overweight man in a rumpled business suit perched on a stool.

As they walked in, all eyes focused on them for a moment. Kane knew his 6'4" frame cut an imposing figure, and Traynor wasn't much smaller. Add in the fact that they were accompanied by a beautiful woman and it was just about impossible for them not to turn heads.

But it wasn't just that, Kane knew. It was also the way they involuntarily radiated primal violence that captured attention. On some subconscious level, everyone in the room sensed that warriors had just entered their vicinity.

Traynor pointed to a couple in the far corner, huddled at one of the tables. "There's Mike."

They were both nursing beers, but to Kane, they looked like they needed something with a lot more kick to deal with the misery etched on their haggard faces.

The bar returned to normal noise levels as the team approached.

Traynor gave Reardon's hand a firm shake. "Good to see

you, Mike. How's it going?" He immediately shook his head. "Sorry, man, stupid question."

Reardon weakly smiled away the faux pas and gestured to the woman sitting beside him. "You remember my wife Becky?"

"Of course," said Traynor. "Good to see you, Becky."

She was a thin, plain-looking woman with shoulder-length brown hair and a mousy demeanor. Her red-rimmed eyes betrayed recent bouts of crying. "I hope you don't mind me tagging along," she said. "After what's happened, I just don't like to be alone."

Traynor nodded. "Perfectly understandable."

He introduced them to the rest of the team. They took their seats, ordered beers, and got right down to business. Everyone at the table knew this wasn't a social call that required small talk and chitchat.

Thurston cut right to the chase. "Mr. Reardon, please tell me exactly what it is you want from us."

"That's easy," Reardon said. "I want my son back. If the bastards who took him, end up dead in the process, so much the better. But all that really matters is getting Jeremy back."

"I wanted to name him Ichabod after Ichabod Crane from *The Legend of Sleepy Hollow*," Becky offered. "It's my favorite story. But Mike said it would be considered cruel and unusual punishment by the time he reached middle school, so we went with Jeremy instead."

Kane could be cold at times, but he wasn't callous enough to tell her none of that information mattered. Besides, he recognized it for what it was—the nervous babble-speak of a scared mother. "When you contacted Pete," he said, "you indicated you know why your boy was taken, but would only talk about it in person."

Reardon nodded. "I don't know who I can trust."

"Explain."

Reardon said, "I'm not sure how much Pete filled you in, but I oversee undercover ops for the DEA."

"He mentioned it, yeah."

"A few weeks ago, rumors and scuttlebutt from informants started trickling in about dirty agents getting into bed with one of the Colombian cartels to help them establish a cocaine pipeline into the east coast. There was even talk that they had partnered up with some new Islamic terrorist group for some unknown reason. I didn't think much of it—this kind of shit gets tossed around all the time by snitches looking for a payout—but then three days ago, they—" He paused, lowered his head, and swallowed down hard on the lump in his throat. When he looked back up, his eyes glistened with unshed tears. "They took Jeremy." As he said the words, he white-knuckled his beer bottle. Any tighter and the glass would shatter in his hand. "Those bastards took my son. He's only ten years old."

Whatever tears Reardon restrained, his wife more than made up for. They flowed down her cheeks in rivers of liquid grief. She pushed back her chair and stood up. "I'm sorry," she said, voice barely a choked whisper. "Please excuse me."

She fled into the bathroom and just before the door closed, Kane heard her sob. Couldn't say he blamed her. She was a mother with a missing child, and that kind of heartache exceeded anything he could imagine. The scumbags who had inflicted that pain upon her didn't deserve to keep sucking God's good air.

"How do you know your son's abduction had anything to do with this DEA-cartel alliance?" Thurston asked. "Pardon me for being blunt, but kids are taken all the time."

"They took him to make me talk. They sent me a note the next day," Reardon replied. "They think we've got someone undercover in the cartel, and they want me to give up the name, or they'll kill Jeremy."

"Is there a UC?"

"If there is I didn't put him there."

"So you don't even have a name to give them if you wanted to."

Reardon made a hopeless gesture with his hands. "Exactly. There's nothing I can do to get my son back." He looked pointedly at Kane. "But if what I've heard is true, you guys can."

At that moment, Kane heard the click of the bathroom door unlocking. At the same time, the bar's front door opened and three skeleton-masked men in long coats barged in and whipped out a quartet of Micro-Uzis.

"Down!" Kane flipped the wooden table and drew his Sig.

Becky Reardon froze in the bathroom doorway and screamed.

"Becky!" Mike yelled.

Kane threw himself toward the woman.

He hit the floor at Becky's feet as the machine-pistols cut loose. As he skidded to a stop against the fat man's barstool, he took out the nearest shooter with a pair of bullets to the face.

Adrenalin thundered in his ears, but he still heard Becky's screams turn into wet gurgles. He looked up and saw her twitching spastically in the bathroom doorway as slugs ripped her open from neck to navel.

Above the roar of automatic fire, he heard Reardon's anguished cry.

The bar was a kill-zone. The air seethed with bullets.

One of the gunners kept Traynor, Thurston, and Reardon pinned down behind the table, steel-jacketed salvos shearing splinters from the wooden surface, hammering relentlessly at the makeshift barrier.

Having executed Becky, the other gunman sprayed the room with indiscriminate fire. The bartender ducked behind the bar, but the patrons had nowhere to go. Streams of lead chopped them down. Death and destruction ruled the night as the blood-spewing victims crashed to the floor.

Since there was nothing he could do for Becky, Kane started to bring his gun back into the game. But just as he went to raise the Sig, the overweight man toppled from the barstool with a 9mm hole between his eyes and pinned Kane's arm beneath his dead weight.

The skeleton-masked attacker turned the Micro-Uzi on Kane, tracking a line of fire towards him. Kane pressed himself as flat as possible behind the corpulent corpse, using the thick body as a shield. He felt the thudding impacts of bullets slamming into dead meat and knew it was just a matter of seconds before some of those bullets punched all the way through and drilled into him.

There was no time to pull his arm free. But he had enough wrist movement to angle the Sig toward the gunman. He stroked the trigger. The bullet skimmed just above the floorboards and smashed into the guy's ankle. Behind the mask, the man howled in pain as bone ruptured into jagged splinters that tore through his flesh like shrapnel. He fell sideways and landed hard on his shoulder.

While the gunman was in mid-fall, Kane wrenched his bruised arm out from under the bullet-ripped corpse. By the time the guy hit the floor, Kane was already on the trigger. A tight-grouped triple-burst sheared off the top of the man's head.

On his peripheral, he glimpsed Reardon low-crawling toward Becky, who was sprawled in the bathroom doorway like a blood-soaked rag doll. Her lifeless eyes stared straight ahead into whatever awaited beyond the business end of a bullet.

The last gunner swiveled toward Kane, apparently perceiving him as the most immediate threat. But without his comrades for backup, the man was woefully outgunned. The second his fusillade stopped hammering the over-turned table, Traynor and Thurston popped up like pistol-packing jack-in-the-boxes and smoked him in his tracks. The guy died hard, head and chest punched full of holes.

Kane rolled onto his back as Reardon slumped against the bullet-shattered jukebox, clutching his dead wife in his arms, uncaring about the blood getting all over him. Grief twisted his face into an agonized rictus. "No, no, no," he kept saying as if repeating the word over and over would somehow bring her back. "No, no, no, oh God, please, no..."

Kane climbed to his feet and put a hand on the DEA agent's shoulder. "Sorry, man." He left it at that. There was nothing more to say, no words to ease the agent's pain.

He walked over to his teammates. His right arm ached from being pinned under the dead man's weight, but other than that, he was fine.

Traynor's eyes burned with anger. "Tell me we're going after the sons of bitches that did this. Tell me we're gonna find his boy."

Sirens sounded in the distance as Kane looked at Thurston. "Your call, boss."

Thurston's pretty brown eyes did nothing to betray her thoughts as she studied the weeping Reardon for a moment. But a slight tightening of her jaw gave away some of the emotions brewing behind her otherwise impassive face. She abruptly pulled her gaze back to Kane and Traynor. "Cops will be here soon. You two better bug out. I'll hang back, clear things up with the authorities, and meet you back at the airport."

Her eyes returned to Reardon, his tears spilling into his wife's hair as he held her close and murmured her name again and again like a litany of grief. In a voice both soft as silk and hard as steel, she said, "Oh, and gentlemen? You can bet your asses we're going after these bastards."

CHAPTER 2

Due to the fluctuating timetables of the targets, the three terrorist attacks didn't happen in perfect synchronicity, but they all happened on the same day within hours of each other. When Jack Carter, the President of the United States, entered the Situation Room for his first briefing on the triple-pronged strikes, he commented, "Ladies and gentlemen, I think we can rule out coincidence."

———

The Atlantic Ocean

Ned Tarkinson had captained the *Norwegian Gem*, a Jewel-class ship for the Norwegian Cruise Line, out of the Manhattan Cruise Terminal at least fifty times in the last three years. Hell, he probably could have done it half-drunk and with one eye closed, but that would never happen because Tarkinson took great pride in his nautical duties. He always looked the part of a captain, his uniform clean, pressed, and sharply creased.

Since taking command of the *Norwegian Gem,* he'd never had a serious incident, nothing beyond the usual seasickness (why the hell did people prone to motion sickness book cruises?) and the occasional got-drunk-and-fell-down injury. In fact, the top cruise review sites on the internet rated him as one of the safest captains working the ships today.

On this sunny late June morning, Captain Tarkinson had no idea that his impeccable safety record was about to suffer some serious damage. *Permanent* damage.

They were three hours out to sea, headed for the south Caribbean at twenty knots, with just over two thousand passengers on board. The Atlantic was calm, the sailing smooth, and the gulls wheeled overhead with their distinctive cries. Captain Tarkinson looked forward to strolling the decks later, mingling with the guests so he could savor the crisp, clean smell of the salt air, which he considered the greatest scent in the world.

He heard the metallic buzz of the Cessna 172's motor a few seconds before the single-engine plane spiraled down in a twisting kamikaze dive and slammed into the bridge at what seemed like 200 mph. Most of the crew were killed immediately, bodies crushed and mangled. Those lucky enough to survive the initial impact were only lucky for another split second, then the hundred pounds of Semtex that had been packed into the plane's cargo hold exploded. The blast blew the bridge—and everyone in it—to shattered rubble. Fiery debris and torn body parts rained down on the lower decks as the passengers screamed and panicked. Burning aviation fuel sent flames racing among the wreckage as smoke billowed into the sky.

Two minutes later, four unmarked speedboats appeared, throttles wide open, racing toward the damaged cruise ship. Each boat was piloted by a single person. Some of the *Norwegian Gem*'s passengers pointed and cheered as the vessels raced toward them, thinking they were rescued. They had no idea how wrong they were.

Dead wrong.

The speedboats were not salvation. They were damnation, ridden by suicidal zealots and Semtex. Though nobody on the crippled cruise ship could hear it over the crackle of the flames, the panicked screams of the passengers and the high-speed whine of the boats' engines, all four pilots chanted three words as they closed in on their target.

"Bin Laden rises! Bin Laden rises!"

Their cryptic last words. In their final seconds of life, they raised fists clenched in victory. Then all four boats slammed into the port side of the ship at almost exactly the same time and erupted into fireballs of destruction, tearing gaping holes in the ship's hull. A quarter-ton of Semtex made for one hell of an explosion, and the cruise ship was rocked, shuddering like a mortally wounded whale. Water flooded into the jagged, blackened holes. Almost immediately, the *Norwegian Gem* listed to port as it began to sink toward the bottom of the Atlantic, dragged down by the invading water as surely as if sucked into the murky depths by the giant tentacles of a prehistoric squid.

With the bridge destroyed, there was no com left to call for assistance, and this far out to sea, there was no cell service. Stranded, sinking, and under attack, the passengers were on their own. Eventually, they figured out how to release the lifeboats, but without a captain to lead them or anyone stepping up to take charge, the boarding was absolute mayhem, a chaotic mess of pushing and shoving. Fueled by desperation, their survival instincts causing their primal, more bestial natures to slip through the fissures, people fought each other. Fistfights broke out as passengers tried to battle their way to the front of the mob. More people ended up in the ocean than in the boats. Wailing children floated in their lifejackets like little bobbers while anguished parents screamed their names.

Once the ship had almost completely sank, two more speedboats appeared, nearly identical to the ones that had committed the suicide run earlier. Not knowing if they were friend or foe, the desperate passengers still waved furiously for help. Two of the lifeboats capsized, dumping even more people into the Atlantic. Spitting, sputtering cries echoed across the unfeeling water as the bombing victims struggled to keep from drowning, flailing arms reaching out toward the incoming speedboats, begging to be rescued.

Instead, the boats surged forward as the throttles redlined and plowed straight through the survivors. In addition to the pilot, each boat held three men dressed in traditional Middle Eastern garments and armed with submachine guns. As the vessels ripped through the mass of floating victims, propellers shredding flesh, the gunmen opened fire.

It was the proverbial fish in a barrel slaughter.

This far out to sea, there was no reason for the terrorists to use suppressors. The chattering of the submachine guns cutting loose on full-auto drowned out the passengers' horrified screams as bullets chopped them into bloody chum for the sharks. Hot brass casings spewed from ejection ports and sizzled when they hit the water, floating on the waves like all the other death debris.

The boats circled like predators, picking off the flailing, screaming, splashing people desperately trying to swim away from them. The terrorists killed as many as they could, and when their magazines ran empty, scores of corpses riddled with gaping wounds bobbed grotesquely on the waves.

The two boats raced away from the carnage before the fast-sinking cruise ship could suck them down in its vortex. They were murderers, not martyrs. Those who wished to sacrifice themselves in the name of Allah had already done so, in glorious fashion, no doubt already reaping their rewards in paradise. The gunmen in the speedboats had merely wished to kill for the cause. They felt called to spill infidel blood, not shed their own.

When they got back within signal range, one of the terrorists took out a burner phone and typed out a two-word text to a contact named Johnny.

MISSION ACCOMPLISHED

He hit "Send."

———

La Guardia Airport
New York City

The Bombardier Learjet 31A raced down the runway and lifted off into the sky. The two-man flight crew had filed a flight plan that would shuttle the family of six on board down to the Florida Keys for a weeklong vacation. The eleven-year-old girl with the pink bow in her ponytail was very excited. Her father had promised to take her swimming with the dolphins.

As the Learjet banked over Bowery Bay, a man stood up in a small motorboat and braced his feet for balance as he shouldered a surface-to-air missile launcher. He did not have extensive training with the weapon, but he had enough to send the missile rocketing up into the sky where it chased down the heat signature from the Bombardier's engines. The jet exploded in a brilliant orange fireball, streams of burning aviation fuel shooting in all directions like a deadly starburst.

As the flaming debris and mangled body parts rained down into the waters of the bay, the man dropped the launcher over the side of the boat. He watched it sink for a second, then pulled out his burner phone, thumbed through the handful of contacts until he found Johnny, and hit "send" on a pre-typed text.

MISSION ACCOMPLISHED

He tossed the phone overboard. It made a small splash and then sank like a stone, vanishing into the water's depths. Then he waited. This close to the airport, escape would be impossible. Already emergency vehicles were racing down the runway toward him, sirens sounding their banshee wail. Not too far in the distance, a blue-and-white police boat raced toward him, foam churning in its wake. He could see officers bracing themselves against the chop, AR-15 carbines bristling in their hands. After what he had just done, their trigger fingers would be itchy.

A police helicopter swooped overhead, then swung around to hover about fifty meters off his port bow. The rotor wash whipped up spray from the river. The terrorist felt like he was standing in the rain, his clothes getting soaked. Not that it mattered; he wouldn't need them much longer.

The police boat arrived on the scene, zagging to his right to take up position off his starboard. The three officers on board had their rifles trained on him. He didn't need to see the selector switches to know none of the guns were on "safe."

The time had come.

He reached down into the bottom of his boat, flipped back the tarp laying there, and picked up the AK-47 that had been concealed beneath. A thirty-round banana clip protruded from the weapon like some obscene, deadly growth. As he raised the rifle, he heard one of the officers on the police boat yell, "He's got an AK!"

As he pulled the trigger and fired a salvo up toward the helicopter, he shouted, *"Allahu Akbar!* Bin Laden rises!" He shouted the phrase again as his bullets sparked off the chopper's landing struts, forcing it to bank away and retreat to a safer distance. And then he shouted it again as the cops cut loose with their AR-15s and punched him full of holes with controlled bursts of fire.

Even as the bullets slammed into him, he stretched out his arms in a cruciform martyr's pose and continued to scream his battle cry, until finally one of the 5.56mm projectiles ripped through his head, silencing him forever.

————

Central Park
New York City

On a warm, sunny June lunch hour, it was expected that hundreds of people would gather at Central Park's Sheep Meadow, many of them spreading blankets and settling down for a picnic feast. Others flew kites, read books, or played Frisbee. It was a place folks came for a respite from the sometimes-choking congestion of the city.

Nobody paid the two interracial couples—Middle Eastern men and Caucasian women—any mind when they leisurely strolled into the southeast corner of the meadow, each of them carrying a large wicker picnic basket with wooden handles. They were young, non-threatening, and appeared to be college students taking a break from their studies to soak up some sun. The men were handsome, the girls were pretty, and by most standards, they would be considered attractive couples. They laughed as they walked, feet swishing through the lush grass, and nobody around them sensed anything out of the ordinary.

That all changed when the foursome dropped down on one knee beside their picnic baskets, flipped open the lids, and pulled out matching .45 caliber MAC-10 submachine guns. No suppressors; they couldn't care less if anyone heard the guns' killing chatter.

As the weaponized quartet began shouting, "*Allahu Akbar!* Bin Laden rises!" nearby park visitors started scrambling for their lives and screaming in horror. They stampeded for safety, but for many of them, it was too late.

Elbows braced on their supporting knees for better control, the terrorists opened fire, fingers clamping down on the triggers as they unleashed auto-fire hell.

In addition to delivering .45 caliber rounds at 1,080 feet per second, the MAC-10s featured a notoriously rapid cyclical rate. They cooked off a thirty-round magazine in 2-3 seconds on full-auto, among the fastest SMGs on the planet. But the four killers had prepared for that; instead of bread, wine, and deli meats, each picnic basket contained a dozen fully-loaded, max-capacity magazines. There might not be any lunch in the baskets, but there was a buffet of bullets. As the mags emptied, each terrorist performed a quick exchange and resumed firing. It would be quite some time before they ran out of ammunition. They had come stocked to kill.

The MAC-10s were not precision weapons, and the gunners did not attempt to use them as such. Knowing the limitations of their firepower, they went for the "spray-n'-pray" method of saturating the target area with as many high-velocity slugs as possible. The goal was maximum death, maximum carnage.

The bullets scythed through soft flesh, ripping into the mob of fleeing people with a brutal lack of mercy. The lethal projectiles made no distinction between men, women, and children—all went down like stalks of wheat before a threshing machine. Not even baby strollers were spared the full-auto fusillade as the four terrorists gunned down innocents in the name of their unforgiving god. Parents screamed as the newly-born became the newly-dead.

Blood flew everywhere as the terrorists smiled cruelly, relishing the slaughter. Hot brass spewed in metal streams from the SMGs' ejection ports, sunlight gleaming on the spent casings as they scattered all over the grass.

It took just three minutes to exhaust all the magazines. One hundred and eighty seconds of death and destruction and chaos. By the time the final bullet buried itself in human flesh, sixty-two people lay dead. The oldest was an eighty-nine-year-old great-grandmother; the youngest, a month-old infant.

The only person to fight back was the infant's father, who held his dead daughter with one arm while he pulled a Glock and returned fire with anguished tears streaming down his face. He just barely grazed one of the female terrorists in the shoulder before her companions shredded him—and his child's body—to pieces with converging lines of auto-fire.

Sirens banshee-wailed in the distance as they fled the scene. They took the MAC-10s with them but left behind the slew of spent cartridges. They had donned latex gloves while filling the magazines, so there were no fingerprints on the brass.

In their pre-staged getaway car—mocked up to look like a taxi in order to blend in with all the cabs clogging the city streets—one of the men palmed his burner phone and opened his messaging application. His hands shook so badly from adrenalin aftermath that he could barely type out the text to Johnny, the mastermind of the attack, the orchestrator of the carnage, the one to whom they had sworn allegiance.

MISSION ACCOMPLISHED

He hit send, and then they went back to their shared apartment and engaged in a fierce, primal four-way orgy, reveling in raw lust to celebrate their blood-soaked victory over the infidels as they awaited their next assignment. During the carnal indulgence of naked flesh, both women closed their eyes and imagined it was Johnny thrusting between their spread-eagled thighs, that it was Johnny's mouth hungrily devouring their breasts. And in the end, when they screamed their release, it was Johnny's name they cried out.

———

The object of their fantasies, the charismatic man known as Johnny Jihad, sat in his safe-house and smiled with every "MISSION ACCOMPLISHED" text he received. He had let loose his dogs of war, and they had fulfilled his bloody vision. He had scarcely dared to believe that he could actually pull off his masterplan. And while the Quran warned against exalting oneself, he couldn't help but feel a swelling of pride at what he had accomplished. Years of work, years of recruiting, years of planning... it had all come together, and it was goddamned glorious.

Johnny felt no shame, no sense of sinfulness, at saying—or in this case, thinking—the word "goddamned." He was not your typical Mideast Muslim, the kind you see straight out of Hollywood central casting, all swarthy-skinned with heads wrapped in turbans. Rather, he was as American as apple pie, baseball, and copping feels from short-skirted cheerleaders under the bleachers. His hair was blonde enough to qualify for Hitler's master race back in World War II, his skin a well-tanned white, and the only thing on his head was a backwards baseball cap sporting the New York Yankees logo. He drank alcohol, used profanity, got laid when the need arose, and generally acted more like a frat boy than a true follower of Islam.

But while Johnny eschewed the rigid rules and regulations of the faith, his belief and devotion were absolute. He lived for one goal and one goal only—to raise Al-Qaeda to its former glory, to engineer the resurrection that would see the Al-Qaeda network once again publicly proclaimed as the premier global terrorism threat. No longer would they be old news, an afterthought, a tragic but brief page in the history books. They would yet again be a relentless force to be reckoned with, faithful *jihadists* holding merciless blades to the soft, vulnerable, infidel throat of the American way of life.

Following the death of Osama Bin Laden—or rather, the *murder* of Bin Laden—Al-Qaeda had crawled back into obscurity while ISIS started grabbing all the headlines. News agencies around the world declared them to be brutal, barbaric, and possessed by savagery that made them even worse than Al-Qaeda.

Johnny found the thought laughable. Fuck ISIS. They

were a bunch of idiotic assholes who weren't fit to carry Osama's jockstrap. They were all brute force, no brains, no strategy beyond *kill-kill-kill*. Any numbskull barbarian could hack someone's head off and stream the decapitation on the internet. All you needed was a sharp knife and the willingness to get your hands bloody. But to pull off multi-target strikes like he had to today? To synchronize a series of attacks within hours of each other? That took skill, planning, intelligence—and boulder-sized balls. The same skills, planning, intelligence, and balls that Bin Laden had exhibited back when he brought down the towers.

The attacks today were on a level not seen since the September 11, 2001 devastation. Once he claimed the strikes in the name of Al-Qaeda, the news channels would pick it up and put it on twenty-four-hour rotation for the next several days. Damn near every television set in the U.S. would be tuned in. Newscasters, morning show hosts, analysts, and talking heads of all types and persuasion would spend countless hours debating the old attacks versus the new. There would be graphs and archived footage and endless comparisons. And with every utterance of the terrorist organization's name, Al-Qaeda would seep—or rather, be sledgehammered—into America's consciousness. ISIS' name wouldn't be heard for months, maybe even years, or even never again if Johnny had his way.

Those ISIS bastards were bush league. Nothing more than amateurs with AKs and hyperactive bloodlust. Al-Qaeda was the true chosen warrior of Allah, and Johnny intended to ram that truth down America's throat once again. The New Babylon would fall to her knees before Johnny Jihad and his holy fighters.

His real name wasn't Johnny Jihad, of course. Hell, it wasn't even Johnny, for that matter. But he refused to even think about the name his fundamentalist Christian parents had given him. Johnny Jihad was the avatar he had created when he started frequenting Al-Qaeda message boards on the dark web, and it had stuck. He had to admit it had a nice ring to it, rolling off the tongue slick and smooth, yet laced with jagged danger.

He had been fifteen when the towers crumbled. Rather than weep and wail and cry out to a God who clearly didn't give a crap, he had been awestruck by the power Al-Qaeda wielded. He soon rejected his Christian faith—and was in turn rejected and thrown out of the house by his parents, who exhibited Jehovah's love and grace by declaring no heathen Muslim was welcome under their roof—and converted to Islam.

But not the tame, modernized, non-offensive version of Islam. He had no interest in that fluffy fake crap. He went full-on, radicalized militant, embracing a message of violence as the path forward for the faith. He was consumed by a righteous fire that made him want to slay the unbelievers. Leave the mercy and compassion and love-thy-enemies crap to Jesus and the hypocritical pricks who rode a pew on Sunday and sinned like Satan the rest of the week. As far as Johnny was concerned, the only thing Allah cared about was infidel blood. Paradise was the reward, and the way there was red rivers of slaughter.

His violent online rhetoric eventually caught the attention of Al-Qaeda bigwigs in Pakistan. They tutored him, molded him, taught him not just the ways of their faith, but the ways of a warrior, of a *jihadi*. After he spent four months in a Pakistani training camp, followed by a two-month stint at a training camp in Mexico, they tasked him with forming a sleeper cell in New York City.

Johnny knew damn well how rare it was for a white,

American, formerly Christian man to be trusted with such a task. Rarer than finding diamonds in dog shit. But he had the good looks of an underwear model, the high-wattage charisma of a snake-oil TV evangelist, the kind of natural magnetism that made people want to join his cause, and a near-genius ability to use social media savvy to build his flock. He was everything Al-Qaeda could have hoped for, and the leaders praised Allah for guiding him to their cause.

In just a few short years, he amassed a small army of loyal zealots, fellow militants, ready to do whatever he asked of them, including giving their lives. Sacrificial lambs, willing to die for the faith.

But then his handlers told him to just sit and wait.

Johnny remembered thinking, *Are you kidding me?*

He gave it a couple of years, but when nothing happened, and they just kept telling him to be patient, he decided to take matters into his own hands. He was meant for more than just sitting in a cramped room with his keyboard, spewing jihadist jargon into cyberspace.

He had drafted a bold plan, then forged the necessary alliances to put the plan into action, and now enjoyed the financial backing he needed to bring the country to its knees once again. Money was power, and he had both. The attacks would continue until America renounced its false gods. The whores and sinners of the New Babylon would once again face the wrath of the true believers. It would start in New York City but then spread across the nation like an apocalyptic virus.

Al-Qaeda would be resurrected.

America would burn in a righteous conflagration.

And Johnny Jihad would dance in the holy flames.

CHAPTER 3

Team Reaper Headquarters
El Paso, Texas

The Team Reaper headquarters were nothing special to look at. Just a converted warehouse retrofitted with some offices, a briefing room, showers, bunks, etc. In the back of the warehouse were an indoor pistol range and an armory. Despite possessing state-of-the-art equipment and weaponry, the team didn't feel the need for a high-tech base of operations. They were all about hitting hard and fast, taking the battle to the enemy, and they didn't need anything slick and fancy for that.

Once Thurston got back from doing damage control in New York City, she headed for the bunks, scheduling a briefing for 1200 hours. Kane was chomping at the bit to get moving on this mission and find the kid, but he knew the importance of rest. They could all bull their way through sleep deprivation when necessary, but it dulled the senses, clouded the mind. Thurston would be a better, sharper commander after she grabbed some shuteye.

The team assembled in the briefing room at noon, most of them slugging down some sort of caffeinated beverage, be it coffee or soda. When Brooke Reynolds, the team's UAV operator showed up with bags full of takeout burgers, she was hailed a hero. Everybody grabbed one, and when Richard 'Brick' Peters stopped complaining about pickle juice soaking into his bun, they buckled down to business.

Thurston recapped the previous night's events for those not in the know, bringing everyone up to speed, then finished up by saying, "We are absolutely taking this mission. No way in hell can we turn a blind eye to an alliance between rogue DEA agents and the cartels. That's some seriously bad news, and we're going to put a stop to it. And while we're at it, we are going to get Jeremy Reardon back to his father."

Assuming he's still alive, Kane thought but kept it to himself.

"And avenge his mother," Traynor said. "There has to be payback for that."

"That's fine," said Thurston, "but taking down this alliance is our first priority, and rescuing the boy is our second priority." Her dark eyes swept the room, making sure she had everyone's attention. "Vengeance is a distant third."

"As long as it's on the list," Traynor muttered. "Somebody ordered that hit, and I want them dead."

Thurston's gaze bored into him. "You knew Becky Reardon personally. If that's messing with your head, do the right thing and say so now."

"What's that supposed to mean?" Traynor asked.

"Can you stay professional or do you need me to pull you off this assignment?"

"I can't believe you're asking me that."

Kane was leaning against the wall, arms folded. "It's a legitimate question, Pete. Answer it. She needs to know."

"She already knows."

"She needs to hear you say it."

Traynor met Thurston's gaze and said, "I'm cool. You don't need to pull me off."

She looked at him long and hard, then nodded curtly. "Fine... for now. But if I think your desire for payback is compromising this mission, I'll yank your ass so fast you'll be riding the bench before you even realize you're out of the game."

Traynor nodded. "Message received, loud and clear."

Kane pushed away from the wall. "So how do we want to play this?"

"That's your call to make," Thurston replied. "Got any suggestions?"

"A street blitz," Kane said. "Identify some targets, kick some ass, and ask some hard questions until someone coughs up the answers we need."

He had given it a lot of thought on the flight back to Texas. According to Reardon, some renegade DEA boys had stuck their dirty fingers into a narcotics pipeline. But pipelines came with one major weakness: they have a beginning, and they have an end and therefore can be run to ground by someone with the balls for the job. And Team Reaper definitely had the balls.

And the firepower.

Kane reckoned it was time to invade the savage world of white death and start pumping lead into poison-peddlers until someone spilled their guts about a DEA-cartel alliance. Then they could scorch their way up the pipeline until it was nothing but smoking ash and Jeremy Reardon was back in his father's arms.

"So where do we start?" Cara Billings asked. The team's armorer looked like she hadn't slept much. Kane secretly wished he was the reason she had been up all night, but the reality was, they probably wouldn't share a bed again anytime soon. They had both agreed it was for the best. But sometimes he wasn't so sure.

"I can access the DEA's database and supply you with a couple of suspected targets to hit in the NYC area," Sam 'Slick' Swift answered He was the team's resident computer genius, the man with the golden fingers. The current rumor floating around was that he had once belonged to the notorious hacker group Anonymous, but he would neither confirm nor deny. When asked, he would just smirk, shake his head, and ignore the question.

Kane looked over at Thurston. "Has Jones signed off on this?" General Hank Jones was the Chairman of the Joint Chiefs, an ex-Ranger who had served in 'Nam, and the man overseeing the World Wide Drug Initiative. Reaper answered to Thurston, Thurston answered to General Jones, and Jones answered to the President.

She nodded. "I called him on the flight. He said best of luck, handle it as we see fit, let him know if we need anything, and he would keep the President informed."

"That's what he always says."

"Do you want him to say something different?"

Kane grinned. "He could say kick ass and kill 'em all. That'd work for me."

Thurston gave a little smile. "Isn't that what you do anyway? I wasn't aware you were waiting for permission."

"Hey, I let that son of a bitch Montoya live after our first go-round, and it turned into a royal clusterfuck." He shook his head. "Hit 'em hard, put 'em down, and make damn sure they don't get back up."

"Great motto," Cara said. "I want it on a bumper sticker."

"So, when do we start kicking doors?" asked Axel 'Axe' Burton, sounding as eager as a kid begging to visit the candy store. The rough, tough ex-recon marine sniper loved the rush of combat almost as much as he loved the ladies. He was all about the bullets and babes. Getting wounded on the team's first mission in Guatemala hadn't tempered his enthusiasm—for war or women—either. He was happiest with a gun in one hand and a hot chick in the other.

"Give me thirty minutes, and I should have a target for you," said Swift, cracking his knuckles. "Just need to let my fingers work their magic."

"That sounds like one of Axe's lines," Cara said with a grin.

As everyone chuckled, Thurston called out, "You heard the man. Take a break and be back here in thirty."

As the briefing broke up, Kane watched with a smirk as Axe and Reynolds peeled off and headed for the bunks. Nothing like a pre-combat quickie to calm the nerves. They pretended to be discreet, but everyone knew the two operators were having a casual relationship. It was an on again/off again thing with them since Axe wasn't the kind of man to let himself be tied down to just one woman. Kane wasn't exactly sure how Reynolds felt about that, but the couple seemed to genuinely enjoy each other's company when they were together. Kane's policy was not to interfere in team members' personal business as long as they did their jobs.

He headed to the indoor shooting range for some 9mm therapy. Some people practiced yoga to relax, some indulged in a hot bath and a good book, but he preferred to punch holes in paper targets. He had cooked three magazines through his Sig when he sensed someone behind him. He had a good guess who it was.

He turned his head, his peripheral vision picking up Cara leaning against the wall. Her pose caused one hip to thrust out, making her look sexier than she probably realized. Or hell, maybe she knew exactly how she looked.

He put down the pistol and pulled off his ear protection. "Hey," he greeted. "How was Maine?"

Her teenaged son Jimmy, along with Kane's comatose sister Melanie, were hidden away in Maine for their protection. Cara and Kane visited them as often as they could, but it was never enough to ease their guilty consciences. Their jobs, the team, the missions, kept them away from their loved ones longer than either wanted. Cara had spent the last few days there, before being summoned back to headquarters.

"It was a good visit," she said. "Too short, of course, but they always are."

"How's Jimmy?"

"Doing good. He's got that teenage sarcasm and eye-roll down to a science." She paused. "I checked on Melanie too. She's doing... well, you know."

"Yeah," Kane said, with just a trace of bitterness. "She's doing okay for being in a coma."

"You can't give up hope, Reaper."

"I'm not," he replied. "When it comes to my sister, hope is all I'm holding onto."

A long silence followed as they shared a quiet moment, each understanding the other's emotional pain, the internal struggle, the burden of sacrifice.

Finally, Kane asked, "So what brings you down here?"

"Just thought maybe we should talk."

"About what?"

"Don't play stupid with me, Reaper. It doesn't suit you."

"I'm not sure there's anything left to say, Cara."

She looked him in the eye, and he glimpsed the longing there, a scarcely-visible flame that flickered with conflicted desire. "Just tell me you miss it sometimes," she said. "Tell me you miss me. You miss *us*."

"We both agreed it was for the best. You change your mind on that?"

"No." She said it too quickly, then added in a much softer voice, "Sometimes."

Kane stepped in close to her, near enough to feel the magnetic heat between them. He wondered if their mutual attraction would ever fade. In some ways, it would make things so much simpler. Then again, matters of the heart were never simple.

He reached up and gently caressed her cheek, then let his hand drift down to settle on her shoulder. She didn't move away from his touch, nor did she move toward him. "No matter what, Cara, I promise I'll always be there for you. You call, I'll come running."

Her pretty face stared up at him. "Friends, then."

"Yeah, friends," he echoed, then grinned. "Just without benefits."

She grinned back and gave him a wink. "Says who? Why should Axe and Reynolds have all the fun?"

Kane walked over and patted the shooting bench, brushing away the spent cartridges. "So hop your sweet stuff on up here and let's get down to business. You know I shoot better when I get some."

She laughed, pushed away from the wall, and sauntered toward the door. "Nice try, hotshot. See you back in the briefing room."

Kane watched her—well, watched her backside, and he

knew damn well she was giving it some extra sway on purpose—until she disappeared. He felt his body respond and call him a fool for letting her get away. With a deep sigh, he donned his ear protection, threw up a fresh target, and dumped six more magazines downrange. As a stress reliever, it wasn't quite as good as getting naked with Cara, but it got the job done.

When he walked back into the briefing room, several of the monitors had been activated, tuned to various news channels. The team members watched information regarding the terrorist attacks stream in, horror and anger etched on their faces. Nobody even teased Axe and Reynolds about being freshly showered.

"My God," Brick said in shock. "It's nine-eleven all over again."

As if on cue, a talking head appeared on one of the screens to announce that the triple-pronged strike was the worst attack on American soil since the 2001 tragedy. A multicolored bar graph comparing the death tolls appeared.

Kane glanced at Thurston. Her mouth was set in a grim line as she watched the news footage. "We getting involved with this?" he asked.

"Negative," she replied. "You know the rules of the game. Unless it's got cartel fingerprints on it, we don't touch it."

"In other words, stay in our lane," Axe grumbled.

"I'd make an exception to go hunt the assholes who did that," Kane said, pointing at the screen where footage of the debris from the cruise ship massacre was playing over a reporter's remarks that recovery efforts were difficult due to the amount of sharks in the water, drawn there by the thousands of corpses. Another channel ran a shaky cell phone recording of the Central Park slaughter. If there was a video of the jet explosion, nobody had released it yet.

"I think we all would," Thurston replied, "but our mission remains unchanged. We need to take down this DEA-cartel alliance and get that little boy back."

"Doing a blitz is going to be little dicey now," Kane said. "The city is going to be on edge after getting hit by three terror strikes in a row."

"Dicey or not," Thurston said, "it has to be done. If you get jammed up by the locals or the alphabet soup agencies, we'll get things cleared up."

Kane grinned. "You mean you're not going to disavow any knowledge of our existence?"

"You watch too many movies," Thurston said.

Axe started humming the *Mission Impossible* theme.

With a little smile and a roll of her eyes, Thurston turned to their computer wizard. "What did you come up with, Slick? You identify a target for us yet?"

"Well, yeah, of course," Swift replied, "I only needed three minutes for that. I just wanted to give Axe and Reynolds enough time to finish."

Reynolds blushed while Axe shot him a thumbs-up. "Appreciate that, brother."

"You're a kind soul, Slick," Thurston said. "But can we get down to business now?"

"Sure thing," Swift replied. "Your target is the Devil Dog Saloon. A real shithole down in Queens. A lowlife loser by the name of Eddy Chance hangs out there. Looks like the DEA has been keeping tabs on the guy. The file indicates this Eddy fella might have some street-level knowledge of NYC's narcotics trade. Good a place as any to start the ass-kicking."

"There a picture of this guy in those files?" Kane asked.

"Coming right up." Swift's fingers clacked across his keyboard so fast that it sounded like an M134 minigun in "let 'er rip" mode. A grainy surveillance photo and a much clearer mugshot filled the room's largest monitor. "Also sending copies to your phones for field identification," Swift announced.

Traynor stared at the photos with an *I-can't-believe-I'm-seeing-this* look on his face. "Is that a white guy with dreads?"

"Sure is," Kane said. "We should probably kill him just for that."

"Be doing him a favor."

Thurston called out, "Reaper, pick your blitz team and grab your gear. You're wheels up in ninety minutes."

"Cara, Axe, Brick, Arenas, Traynor," Kane said. "You're with me." He headed for the armory, the others falling in behind. "Time to hunt."

———

New York City

LaGuardia was the closest airport to Queens, but it was completely locked down due to the terrorist attack, with fighter jets scrambled overhead. Despite the tensions and heightened security, Team Reaper managed to secure clearance to land their HC-130 at JFK International Airport. Once on the ground, nobody paid them much attention. The place swirled with activity, personnel and vehicles racing in all directions. They looked like they were just one more team arriving on the scene to assist with the aftermath of the strikes.

Nearly eight hours after the attacks, nobody had yet

claimed responsibility. The world watched and waited, ready to put names, faces, or both to the perpetrators of the horrific strikes. News pundits bandied about a list of the usual suspects with ISIS topping the possibilities, but nobody really knew anything at this point. It was all speculation.

The primary strike team for this segment of the mission consisted of Kane, Cara, and Burton. They would be the ones hitting the streets and unleashing the blitz. Arenas, Traynor, and Brick would stay with the plane as the backup team. Traynor seemed annoyed about sitting out while his friend's son was missing, but Kane didn't give a shit. He didn't run an op based on making people happy. His gut told him that keeping Traynor sidelined, for now, was the right call, so he made it.

The Devil Dog Saloon was a rough joint in a rough part of town, frequented after dark by a rough crowd. Definitely not a place for nuns or sissies, Kane thought.

Good thing nobody on Team Reaper was a nun or a sissy.

Sitting behind the wheel of the tinted-window SUV, Kane toggled his mic. "Reaper One to Reaper Four, you in position?"

"Copy, Reaper One," Axe answered. "Reaper Four is in position." He was prone on the roof of the deserted auto parts store directly across the street from the saloon, providing over-watch behind a sound-suppressed M110A1 CSASS, short for Compact Semi-Automatic Sniper System. The weapon was fully loaded with ten rounds of 7.62x51mm NATO ammunition. He could reach out 800 meters with the rifle if necessary. From the end of the suppressor to the front door of the Devil Dog was less than

60 meters. A shot that close he could make with his eyes closed while eating a sandwich.

Kane looked at Cara, riding shotgun next to him. Shadows played across her face. "You ready?" he asked.

"You know it."

"Let's do this." He toggled his mic again. "Reaper One to Reaper Four, we're on the move."

"Copy that, Reaper One. I've got eyes on."

Kane and Cara exited the vehicle and crossed the street. They were dressed in jeans and loose-fitting light jackets to conceal the Sig-Saur M17s riding on their right hips. Slick had sent them more intel during the flight, so they knew the Devil Dog Saloon was part pool hall, part strip club, part drug den, and one hundred percent unwelcoming to strangers.

Kane figured they would just walk up and introduce themselves.

A big, burly brute with the build of a professional wrestler blocked the entrance. He wasn't quite as tall as Kane, but he was wider, with massive muscles bulging the seams of his leather coat. Probably a steroid freak. He gave Cara a look that made it clear what he would like to do with her—or rather, *to* her—and then fixed his stony eyes on Kane. "You're in the wrong neighborhood, boy. Unless you want someone to pull a train on your girl's ass while you watch, you'd best just turn around and go back to wherever the fuck you came from." He pulled back the leather jacket to reveal a Smith & Wesson .357 Magnum hanging on his hip to emphasize he meant business. Light from a bug-spackled streetlamp glinted off the stainless steel.

"Big gun you got there," Kane said. "Guess that means you're happy to see me."

The brute scowled angrily. "Okay, asshole, you're outta

here." He reached for Kane with ham-sized fists attached to oak-thick forearms, probably planning on snapping him in two like a dry twig.

Kane abruptly stiff-fingered the man in the throat. He stopped just short of collapsing the cartilage and killing the guy but struck hard enough to make sure he was out of commission for the foreseeable future. As the gagging goon staggered back, Kane pistoned a powerful sidekick into the man's stomach. He put enough force behind the blow that you probably could have pulled his boot-print off the guy's belly. The bouncer doubled over as the air exploded from his lungs. A wicked uppercut ended the fight—well, beating, to be perfectly accurate—by pulping the man's nose like a hammered strawberry and putting the big boy down on the ground, out cold.

Axe's voice came over the com. "Damn, Reaper One, you think you hit him hard enough?"

"He's still breathing, ain't he?"

"Not through that nose, he's not."

"Eyes peeled, Reaper Four," Kane said as he and Cara stepped over the unconscious man sprawled out on the sidewalk like a sack of garbage. "We're going in."

"Copy, Reaper One. I've got the high ground."

Kane and Cara entered the lion's den.

With the night still young, there weren't that many people occupying the Devil Dog Saloon. Kane scanned the bar and ten sets of hostile eyes glared back at him: Eddy Chance, the bartender, four guys playing pool, and another four guys clustered around a table snorting lines of coke. Despite the city's ban on smoking in bars, cigarette fumes clogged the air, the acrid fog laced with the scent of reefer. The stripper pole was empty. Maybe the nude gyrations didn't start until later.

Beer bottles littered the bar, drug paraphernalia littered everything else, and some kind of country-rap hybrid blatted from the jukebox in the corner. Kane had no idea why anyone would voluntarily listen to that crap. He was more of a rock 'n' roll kind of guy.

Eddy Chance occupied a booth to Kane's left, sipping on—of all things—an umbrella drink. The punk was kind of hard to miss with his pasty white skin, greasy dreadlocks, and the loudest Hawaiian shirt in the history of gaudy clothes. The shirt was a fashion abomination. The white-boy dreads just completed the picture of stupidity.

The bartender was a baldheaded steroid machine who looked strikingly similar to the bouncer Kane had KO'd outside. Maybe they had been brothers. He treated Kane to a pissed off scowl that probably would have made the average person soil their shorts and snarled, "Something we can help you with, pal?"

"Looking to chat with Eddy."

"Wrong bar, buddy."

"No, it's the right bar."

"Yeah? What makes you so sure?"

"Because they said the bartender was a big bald bastard who looked like an elephant's dick."

The barkeeper's scowl turned scarlet with rage. "Okay, you shit-talking son of a bitch, it's body bag time for you if you don't waltz your ass right on outta here in about two seconds." He raped Cara with his eyes. "The whore is free to stay."

Cara treated him to a smile that practically dripped with fake sweetness. "You got it all wrong, chump. Whores get paid. I'll fuck up your world for free."

"The only thing getting fucked up around here is you,"

the bartender growled. "Drag your ass outta here before you get hurt, little girl."

"Hold on a sec," Cara said. "I can't hear you." She whipped out her Sig and pumped a couple of rounds into the jukebox, killing the music mid-croon in a burst of sparks. Her smile broadened. "Much better. You were saying?"

The barkeeper cursed. "You're dead, bitch!" He pulled a sawed-off Remington 870 shotgun out from under the counter.

Big mistake.

His *last* mistake.

Kane reached for his Sig as Cara hit the trigger and blasted a trio of red-hot slugs into the barkeep's chest. The 9mm triple-whammy sent the man crashing backwards into the shelves of liquor behind him. Bottles of booze smashed to the floor. Blood mixed with Jack Daniels to form a puddle of gore. Kane thought that was a waste of good whiskey.

The gaggle of guys playing billiards clawed for their hardware as Kane swung his arm up, gun bucking in his fist as fast as he could pull the trigger—and he could pull it pretty damn fast. None of them ducked or dodged, believing they could beat him to the draw.

They were dead wrong.

Kane hammered the first target in the center of his chest. He went down spewing frothy blood from his gasping-fish mouth. The other three joined him in hell a heartbeat later as bullets struck with shattering impact, ripping the lives right out of them.

In the blink of an eye, five tangos down.

The remaining men grabbed for their guns.

One two words could describe them.

Too slow.

Kane and Cara cut them down. Bullets scythed through

bad guys in a blizzard of hot lead. Blood sprayed the air and gave all the cigarette smoke a red tint. Kane punched the ticket of the last man standing, leaving him draped across a table with his brains drizzling all over the lines of coke.

Without missing a beat, Kane swung his gun around and kept it trained on Eddy while Cara performed a tactical magazine exchange, replacing her partially depleted clip with a full one. Always better to have a maxed-out weapon than one half-empty. She then returned the favor and Kane did the same.

The dreadlocked drug dealer hadn't moved so much as an inch during the mayhem. It was like the bench was an electromagnet and his butt made of metal. He now surveyed the chaos and carnage they had conjured up in mere seconds and slowly clapped his hands. "That, man, was pretty damn impressive. You looking for a job? 'Cause I would hire you two in a flat second."

Kane and Cara, guns at the ready, walked over to Eddy's booth. "We don't work for dirtbags," Kane rasped. "We're just here to ask you a few questions, and then we'll be on our way."

"Will I still be alive when you're on your way?" Eddy asked.

"One step at a time," Kane said. "Answer the questions, and we'll go from there."

"That doesn't exactly fill me with comfort."

"Do I look like the kind of guy who gives comfort?"

"You look like the kind of guy that gives enemas by Smith and Wesson." Eddy thrust his chin toward his pastel-colored beverage. "Mind if I take a drink?"

"Go ahead, but I'd make sure your moves are real slow."

Eddy reached for his umbrella drink, took a sip, and let out a contented sigh. "That hits the spot. Just what I needed to wash down all the gun-smoke." He looked up at Kane. "You guys wanna sit down?"

"We'll stand. We're not staying long."

"Let's speed this up," Cara said.

"Go ahead." Eddy brushed a pair of dreads out of his face. "Let's hear your questions."

"You know anything about a DEA-cartel alliance?" Kane asked.

Eddy twirled the umbrella in his drink. "Answering that could be very hazardous to my health."

Kane gestured around the corpse-strewn bar. "Does it look like we're with the Boy Scouts? Not answering the question will be hazardous to your continued existence." He hefted the Sig for emphasis.

"Well, when you put it that way..." Eddy nodded, the dreads writhing around his face like hairy snakes. "All I can give you is the word on the streets. A name, to be precise."

"So, let's have it."

"Dick Mason."

"Who is he?"

Eddy shrugged. "No idea, man. Just heard his name in connection with the alliance you just mentioned."

Cara raised her pistol. "Maybe if I put a bullet in your balls, you'll remember more."

Eddy held up his hands. "Whoa, lady, back up and slow your roll. You know what I know, I swear. You can play with my balls if it'll make you feel better, but it won't get you any more information, 'cause I ain't got any more to give, and that's the God's honest truth."

"God's got nothing to do with this," Kane snapped. "You sure the DEA is in bed with the cartels?"

"I ain't *sure* of anything, man. Just telling you what I've *heard*."

Axe's voice came over the com. "Reaper Four to Reaper One, the guy you left outside is starting to wake up."

"Copy that, Reaper Four. If he makes a move before we get out there, put him down."

Eddy stared at him in disbelief. "Call sign Reaper? Really? Who the hell are you guys?"

"People you don't want to fuck with," Kane replied. "Now, I've got just two more questions."

"Fire away."

"Got any cigarettes?"

"Sure." Eddy reached into the breast pocket of his Hawaiian shirt and pulled out a crumpled pack of Marlboros. He handed the cancer sticks to Kane.

"Thanks." Kane crushed the pack in his fist and dropped it to the floor.

"Hey!" Eddy protested. "What the hell was that for, man?"

"Those things will kill you," Kane said. "Last question—got a light?"

"What do you want a light for? You just jacked up my cigarettes!"

Kane touched off a round. The umbrella drink shattered in a pastel-hued explosion right in front of Eddy, splattering his shirt. "I'm asking the questions, not you."

"Sure. Sure, yeah, okay, no problem. A light. You want a light. Here ya go, man." Eddy produced a Zippo and handed it over.

Without another word, Kane and Cara headed for the door. He toggled his mic. "Reaper One to Reaper Four, we're coming out."

"Copy that, Reaper One," Axe replied. "Be advised, big boy is on his feet at this time."

Kane paused a few steps from the exit and flicked on

the Zippo. The flame danced from the stainless-steel lighter. "You might want to blow town," he said to Eddy.

Eddy's brow furrowed in puzzlement. "Why's that?"

Kane gave him a wolfish smile. "Because things are about to get real hot around here."

With a flick of his wrist, he tossed the Zippo across the room and behind the bar where the broken bottles of alcohol instantly ignited. Flames whooshed to life and began barbecuing the bartender's corpse as the fire spread rapidly. The place would soon smell like burnt meat, but they would be long gone by then.

Eddy yelled, "My bar! You bastard!"

"And then some," Kane rasped.

He opened the door to find the bouncer standing in front of them, swaying on his feet like a punch-drunk boxer, blood pouring from his crushed nose to splatter on the sidewalk. As soon as he saw them, he snarled a curse and reached for his .357 Magnum. He missed on the first grab but got it on the second try.

Before he even cleared leather, Kane buried the toe of his boot in the bouncer's balls, driving his scrotum up against his pelvic bone with crushing force. All sorts of soft, tender tissue ruptured, and the man fell to his knees, a high-pitched wail keening from his shivering lips. The girlish scream got choked off when vomit spewed from his mouth.

Kane powered his knee up into the brute's chin, snapping his head back with enough force to nearly break his neck. The bouncer flipped over backward and crashed down on his spine with a heavy thud, lights out once again, probably dreaming of his new life as a soprano.

Kane and Cara stepped over the bouncer's blacked-out body and climbed into the SUV. Smoke began to billow from the Devil Dog, and they saw Eddy stagger out, coughing and hacking as he stumbled down the sidewalk to safety.

Axe joined them moments later, sliding into the back-seat, and Kane drove off into the night, leaving behind death and flames to mark their passage.

They all knew things were going to get a whole lot hotter before they were done.

————

Kane pulled into an alley, called headquarters, and got Swift on the line. "Need you to run a name for me."

"You finally found a match? I gotta tell you, Reaper, people don't typically use their real names on those hookup sites."

"You're a funny guy, Slick. Are you done?"

"Yeah, sorry." He didn't sound sorry at all. Kane heard a machinegun-like clatter of keys and then: "Okay, give me the name."

"Dick Mason."

"Richard Mason," Swift corrected. "No parent names their kid Dick."

"Yeah, well, plenty of parents raise dicks," Kane said.

"Stop being an old, grumpy, millennial-hating bastard," Swift retorted over the sound of clacking keys. A few seconds later he said, "Bingo. Here we go. Okay, bottom line is that Richard Mason is a nobody, a low-level paper-pusher for the DEA."

"He might be a nobody, but he's got some connection to this alliance crap."

"Or maybe Eddy fed you a load of bull."

"Only one way to find out. Mason based in New York?"

"Yeah. Rockland County. About an hour from your location."

"Give me the address."

"Sending it to your phone now."

"Thanks, Slick."

"No problem, Reaper. Happy hunting."

Kane hung up and dialed Mike Reardon. As he waited for the DEA agent to pick up, he reflected that Slick might be right, that Eddy had played him. But he didn't think so. Eddy Chance was one of those bottom-feeding weasels with a knack for survival, and he had honestly believed Kane would put a bullet in his head. Live to die another day, that was the fatalistic creed of gutter rats like Eddy, so Kane was willing to bet that he had played it straight and told the truth.

When Reardon answered the phone, Kane didn't waste time with chitchat, just got right down to business. They were in blitz mode, hitting hard, moving fast from target to target. Small talk could wait until the mission was over. Hopefully, that small talk didn't take place at the graveside of a young boy. "Mike, it's Reaper. The name Richard Mason mean anything to you?"

"Not off the top of my head. Why? Is he involved in this mess? Does he know where my son is?"

Kane could hear the desperation in the man's voice. "Not sure, but his name popped up on our radar."

"So, what are you going to do?"

"Pay him a visit," Kane said grimly.

———

Rockland County, New York

The Mason home was out in the suburbs. Swift fed them the satellite imagery as they drove up the Palisades Interstate Parkway North, showing nothing more than the average one-family ranch house, complete with a two-car garage and above-ground swimming pool in the privacy-fenced backyard, situated on a well-maintained one-acre lot. It was exactly what you expected a middle-class federal government employee to own.

Had it been normal daylight hours, they could have just walked up and rang the doorbell. But unless they were a fool, nobody would open their door after dark to talk to strangers, not even out here in the suburbs. And it wasn't like Kane and Axe could pass as vacuum cleaner salesmen or Jehovah Witnesses. Tall and broad-shouldered, they both carried themselves like men more suited for war than peace.

So Kane decided to scrap the soft approach and go with a home invasion approach. Axe and Cara remained outside to watch his six, sticking to the deep shadows close to the house. Luckily, rows of pine trees on each side of the property screened them from any prying eyes or nosy neighbors.

Kane slipped quietly through the darkness, edging around the perimeter of the house, seeking a penetration point. All the windows were black except one, soft orange light spilling out into the night. He crouched beneath it, then slowly raised his head to peer through the glass. Through a narrow gap in the curtains, he saw a bedroom lit only by a few candles. On the queen-sized waterbed, he saw a paunchy man and a plump woman gyrating wildly, going at it with gusto and little regard for anything other than their carnal satisfaction. Through the glass, Kane could hear the woman's moans of pleasure and Mason's panting grunts. Candlelight glistened on the sweat streaming down their naked bodies.

Kane grinned. This was going to be too easy. *Coitus interruptus* courtesy of Sig-Sauer.

The slapping of flesh and enthusiastic cries of coupling worked in tandem to cover any sound Kane made as he raised the window and crept into the room. His boots sank into the plush carpet, silent as stepping on a cloud.

He aimed the Sig at the nude man pounding against his partner's rippling flesh. "Hey," he said, raising his voice to be heard over the woman's loud howls of passion. "Quit screwing around and pay attention."

"What the—? Shit!" Mason rolled onto his back, waterbed sloshing like a miniature tsunami. Even in the dim light of the candles, his splayed legs revealed way more than Kane wanted to see. The woman started to scream and clutch the covers to her breasts. Kane had to admit they were pretty impressive.

He expressed his appreciation for the skin show by putting a bullet in the headboard next to her ear. He had no intention of hurting her, but she didn't know that. "Keep your mouth shut," he said. "No reason to scream. I just need to ask your husband a few questions, and then I'll be gone."

She shook her head and pulled the covers all the way up to her chin. "He's not my husband."

"Then who the hell are you?"

"His secretary. His wife's out of town visiting her family."

"Guess that makes him an asshole and you a slut, but that's none of my business."

Mason switched from fearful shock to indignant anger in less time than it takes most people to peel off a used condom. "Who are you?" he demanded. "What the hell is going on? You're making a big mistake, buddy. You can't do this. For god's sake, I'm a federal agent. I have rights, dammit!"

Kane stalked toward him, eyes cold and deadly as a rattlesnake's stare. "Damn straight you have rights," he said. Mason cringed away from the ice-eyed warrior. "You have the right to be silenced if I decide that's the best course of action." He pressed the end of the Sig's suppressor against Mason's wilting manhood. "So start telling me everything you know about the DEA getting in bed with the cartels, or I'll change your name to Dick-*less*."

Turned out Mason wasn't much for holding up under pressure. All it took was a gun to his crotch, and he skipped the denial stage and buckled right down to the blabbing. "I don't know much. I'm a desk jockey. I push paper. That's my job, that's what I do. That's *all* I do. I'm a paper pusher. I noticed a few discrepancies on some forms, asked a few questions, and was paid good money to keep my mouth shut."

Kane didn't interrupt to tell him he was doing a lousy job at that.

"That's the extent of my involvement," Mason finished. "From what I hear, the higher-ups are the ones really getting their hands dirty."

"Way I hear it, they're fist-deep in cartel ass," Kane rasped. "What were the forms?"

"Shipping manifests."

"Cargo ships?"

Mason nodded. "Yeah."

"From where?" Kane asked.

"Colombia."

"So they're bringing the shit in through the ports."

"Easiest way to smuggle coke—or any drugs, for that

matter—as long as you can afford to pay off the DEA and Customs agents."

"Pocket change for a Colombian cartel," Kane said. "Now, give me the names of the higher-ups who are getting their wallets greased."

"I don't know."

Kane rammed the pistol harder against Mason's groin. "Then I don't know if I can keep my finger off this trigger."

"Wait! I can give you the name of the guy who paid me off."

"Better than nothing. Let's hear it."

"Steve Nash." Mason nervously glanced down at the suppressor grinding against his private parts. "The only other name I've heard in regards to this alliance is someone called the Razor."

"The Razor?"

"Yeah." Mason nodded. "I'm guessing it's a nickname."

"Brilliant deduction," Kane drawled sarcastically.

Mason looked up at him nervously. "That's all I know, I swear to God."

Kane probed Mason's eyes for deception, for any indication of a lie. Satisfied that the DEA agent had told the truth, he removed the Sig from Mason's groin. The man let out a long sigh of relief and reached down to cover himself. His secretary remained quivering under the covers, watching Kane with wide eyes and trembling lips.

Kane decided to let Mason go. Plenty of bodies would hit the floor before this was over, but they had bigger fish to fry tonight than some low-level agent paid off to ignore some shady paperwork. Taking down Mason would be the equivalent of pulling a single scale off a snake when you really needed to chop off the whole damn head. They were hunting sharks, not minnows.

Kane gestured toward the Glock 17 lying on the night-stand next to an open tube of Astroglide. "Make a move for that thing, and you'll regret it."

Fool that he was, Mason ignored the warning. As Kane ducked down to climb out the window, the DEA agent apparently felt the need to seek redemption for the way he'd been humiliated. So he grabbed for the Glock.

Big mistake.

Straddling the windowsill, Kane fired a 9mm rocket into Mason's bare ass, the suppressor reducing the shot to a muffled cough. He deliberately placed the bullet to the right of Mason's tailpipe. He was going for incapacitation, not termination; a direct hit would have blown the guy's guts out all over the place. Instead, the bullet tore through the flabby meat of his buttocks and skidded off his hipbone.

Mason lurched forward, banging his skull off the head-board with a brain-jarring thud as blood sprayed across the rumpled sheets. "Oh, you son of a bitch!" he howled. "You son of a *bitch!*" He reached behind him to clutch at the wound with trembling fingers, the Glock forgotten.

"Damn right I'm a son of a bitch," Kane growled. "I suggest you type up a letter of resignation and then get the hell out of town." He slid the Sig back into its holster. "Because if I ever see you again, they'll be carving your name on a gravestone."

As Mason laid there and whimpered, the woman took one look at the bloody wound and fainted. She slumped down, face disappearing under the covers. Kane ignored them both as he faded into the darkness.

CHAPTER 4

On the outskirts of Rockland County, Kane pulled the SUV into a deserted gas station and called headquarters.

Thurston answered and in her usual fashion, got right down to business. "Did you get anything from Mason?"

"Found out he's banging his secretary," Kane replied. "Want the details?"

"I'm guessing they're not pertinent to the mission, but thanks for sharing," Thurston replied. "Anything else?"

"He coughed up a couple of names. Need Slick to run them."

"Yeah, well, it's gonna have to wait. Find a television. The terrorists released a video, and you're not going to believe this shit. Call back when you're up to speed."

She hung up, and Kane quickly found a news channel on his phone. Thurston was right—he couldn't believe what he was he was hearing. "Unbelievable," he muttered, adjusting the angle of the screen so Cara and Axe could see. "Looks like Al-Qaeda's back in business."

Axe shook his head in disbelief. "Are you kidding me?"

he growled. "I thought we put those jerkoffs down for the count."

Grimly, Kane replied, "Looks like they're back from the dead."

———

The White House
Washington, D.C.

President Jack Carter sat in the Situation Room of the White House's west wing and stared angrily at the screen. If a caricature artist could have captured him in that exact moment, they would have drawn him with a red-flushed face and steam shooting out his ears. "I thought these sons of bitches scattered to the four winds after we put a bullet in Bin Laden's brain," he growled.

With him were General Hank Jones, National Security Advisor Kevin McNanes, and CIA Director Russell Quay.

"They never completely folded," McNanes replied. "But they were a shell of what they once were, that's for sure."

Carter pointed at the images of carnage on the screen and scowled. "They came close to killing as many American citizens today as they did on nine-eleven. Three attacks in a single day. That's not the work of a shell, gentlemen."

"Looks like they managed to pull themselves back together," Quay said.

The President tossed him a stern look, his face reflecting his foul mood. "And despite everything we learned after the towers came down, they still somehow managed to hit us again, *in the same damn city,* right under our noses."

On the screen, a man wearing a black, hooded mask was speaking. The caption beneath him simply said "Johnny Jihad." Whoever had filmed the video had focused the camera tight on his face, revealing nothing of his surroundings save for a flag used as a backdrop. Not the traditional black Al-Qaeda flag, but an upside-down American flag that appeared to have been hacked to shreds by a madman with a knife and then splattered with blood. Real or fake, it was impossible to tell from the footage. In the corner, covering the fifty stars, were the words "New Babylon" inside a red circle and slash.

"Today your wretched city again knows fear," Johnny Jihad intoned. "Today you suffered for your grave mistake—the mistake of foolishly believing that you had crushed Al-Qaeda. But today you know the truth—that Al-Qaeda is still very much alive—and with that truth comes death. Death to the infidels, death to the whores, death to all those who would defy Allah!"

President Carter ran his fingers through his gray hair, which was turning even grayer with each passing second. Running the country turned young men old, and he had been old before he even got elected. "This cannot be happening," he sighed.

Nobody responded, all eyes glued to the screen. It was like a horror show you couldn't look away from.

"Today you mourn your dead but do not shed all your tears, for you will need them again tomorrow. You will call me Johnny Jihad, but my name does not matter. What matters is that the spirit of Osama Bin Laden dwells within me and I will bring America, the New Babylon, to her knees once again. I will not cease this holy war until every infidel is burning in hell."

"He's full of crap, right?" President Carter asked.

"Trying to bluff us. He can't really have another attack planned for tomorrow, can he?"

"I wouldn't rule it out," Jones replied. "He planned and executed three attacks. Not too much of a stretch to imagine a fourth."

"Maybe we should lock down the city," McNanes suggested. "Send in the National Guard."

"Easier said than done," Carter said. "There's over eight million people in New York City."

"Evacuation then?"

The President shook his head. "Those that want to evacuate are already doing so. No point in making it mandatory." He pointed at the screen. "Not sure how it gets done, gentlemen, but I want that Johnny Jihad bastard, whoever he is, fitted for a toe tag."

"Not going to be easy," Quay replied. "As you pointed out, he pulled these attacks off right under our noses. The guy's sneaky and clearly knows how to lay low."

With a sour expression on his face, Carter said, "So find whatever hole he's crawled into and drag him out. Pretty sure that's what we pay you to do."

"We can activate some assets if you want to authorize a black bag operation."

"Does your agency have any operations that *aren't* black bag?" President Carter sighed, then added, "Just find him, and this time when you stomp the hell out of Al-Qaeda, make sure they stay stomped. Like bugs under a boot heel, with their guts hanging out."

On the monitor, the terrorist continued to speak, eyes flashing with a zealot's fire from behind the holes in the mask. "There is but one way we will cease our slaughter, our jihad. Only one thing that will make us put down our guns, our blades, our bombs. It will require a great sacrifice from America, perhaps the greatest sacrifice your country has ever had to make."

Johnny paused for effect, then delivered his ultimatum. "There will be no more strikes on American soil if the President of the United States, President Jack Carter, surrenders himself to me for execution."

Jones, McNanes, and Quay all turned and looked at the President.

Carter leaned back in his chair, arched his eyebrows, and said, "Well, ain't that a bitch."

———

Rockland County, New York

Kane, Axe, and Cara watched the video all the way to the end. It ran a little over sixteen minutes and featured the same "kill the infidels, bring America to her knees" nonsense over and over again.

"Johnny boy needs an editor," Cara muttered.

Kane called back to headquarters, putting the phone on speaker. Thurston answered on the second ring. "What do you think?" she asked without preamble.

"They didn't waste any time claiming responsibility," Kane said.

"Yeah, they clearly want us to know Al-Qaeda is alive and kicking."

"Are we even sure it's Al-Qaeda?" Axe asked. "The prick could just be running his mouth."

"I'm sure the CIA will work on authenticating the claim, but they'll take him at his word for now," Thurston replied. "This definitely wasn't a lone wolf scenario. These attacks required significant resources which indicate backing from a terrorist organization."

"Nature abhors a vacuum," Cara commented. "With Bin Laden nothing but shark shit by now, it was only a matter of time until someone stepped in to fill the void. Honestly, I'm surprised it took this long."

"All the counterterrorism analysts predicted Al-Qaeda would fold when Bin Laden bit the dust," Thurston said.

"Cut off the head, and the snake will die," Cara said. "Yeah, I've heard the theory a time or two. Looks like the analysts got this one wrong."

"It happens," Thurston replied. "Nobody's perfect."

"Ballsy," Kane said. "Demanding the President turn himself over to be executed. You gotta know they'd cut his head off and livestream it."

"Ballsy or delusional, take your pick." Thurston sighed. "Either way, it's a nasty bit of business."

"He won't seriously consider turning himself over, will he?" Cara asked.

"You know the policy," Thurston replied. "The United States does not negotiate with terrorists. We all like to think that it's written in stone. But if we get hit by another attack —or, God forbid, multiple attacks—then the American people might start singing a different tune. Trade the life of one President to save the lives of thousands of Americans."

"That's bullshit," Kane said. "He needs to stick to his guns on this."

"He's the President of the United States," Thurston said. "You've met the man, so you know he'll do what he wants, and he's got enough honor in him to make the ultimate sacrifice if he truly believes it will save people."

"It'd be a mistake."

"I don't disagree with you, but it won't be our call to make. Let's just hope it doesn't come to that."

"We being diverted to a jihadi bug hunt?" Kane asked.

"Negative," Thurston replied. "Stay on mission. The President has people to handle terrorists. We focus on cartel assholes."

"Ain't that the truth," Axe cut in. "We've dealt with so many assholes the last few months that I'm thinking we should change our name to Team Proctologist."

"Nah," Cara replied. "Too many syllables."

"If we're gonna keep blitzing," Kane said to Thurston, "then I need Slick to run some names."

"Hold on, I'll patch you through."

A few seconds later, they were connected with Swift. "Greetings from El Paso," the keyboard wizard said. "What can I do you for?"

"Got some names for you to run."

Swift sighed. "You know, Reaper, I'm starting to think you're just using me for my computer." There was a clatter of keys as he pulled up some program.

"You can think what you want, just as long as you give me my intel."

"Thank you for making my point," Swift drawled. More keys got punched, and then he said, "Okay, give me the names."

"Steve Nash and Razor."

"Razor? As in, the shaving utensil?"

"Yeah. You'll probably want to run it as an alias."

"Don't tell me how to do my job, Reaper," Swift warned with exaggerated fierceness. "I don't tell you how to shoot people in the face, and you don't tell me how to run names. This Team Reaper thing doesn't work if we don't all stay in our lanes."

Kane chuckled. "Fair enough, Slick." He lowered his voice. "Thurston near you?"

"Negative. She's in another room."

"Okay. Listen up, Slick. If you get time, take a look at whatever intel is out there on these terrorist attacks, see what you can piece together."

"Not our turf, Reaper. Not even the same neighborhood."

"Yeah, well, even a good dog jumps the fence once in a while and rolls in the mud."

"Fine, but if Thurston catches on to what I'm doing, you're paying my bail."

"I'll make sure it's my ass in the sling, not yours."

"I'm serious, Reaper."

"So am I."

"Okay, then. Grab a powernap. I'll call you when I've got info on Nash and Razor."

Kane hung up to find Cara and Axe staring at him. "What's the problem?"

"You know full well what the problem is," Cara said. "Thurston has operational oversight, and she'll be pissed if she finds out you've got Slick working the terrorist attacks."

"How's she gonna find out? Slick knows how to cover his tracks." Kane's eyes roved back and forth between his two teammates. "You guys gonna tell her?"

Cara shook her head. "I'm not here for telling."

In the backseat, Axe crossed his arms and offered a crooked grin. "I'm good, bro. Snitches get stitches, and I don't want you messing up my pretty face."

"You never know," said Cara. "Some chicks dig scars."

"Did you just call yourself a chick?" Kane asked.

"Hell, no," Cara retorted. "I'm a fucking lady."

The man snarled a curse as his cell phone rang. To her credit, the whore never missed a beat as her head bobbed up and down. Not the best he'd ever had, but what she lacked in skills she compensated for with enthusiasm.

The phone trilled again, intruding on his pleasure. It was his special phone, an untraceable burner, the number known only to a select few. If it was ringing at this time of night, there was nothing but bad news waiting for him. Nobody calls at midnight to say you've won the Publisher's Clearing House Sweepstakes.

All he wanted was to get his rocks off and catch a few hours of sleep before heading to work, but apparently business insisted on taking priority over sexual satisfaction. Better to just take the call and get it over with.

He shoved the hooker's head out of his lap as he answered the phone. "Yeah, what is it?"

"Somebody hit Mason." The voice on the other end of the line didn't bother with an introduction. "Right in his house while he was nailing his secretary."

The man suddenly paid more attention. "Is he alive?"

"Yeah, he's alive. Took a bullet in the ass, though. Nearly got himself a nine-millimeter enema."

"Who did it?" The man's hard-on started to become not so hard. Seeing the onset of flaccidity, the whore reached for him with practiced fingers, but he slapped her hand away like an annoying fly. She crawled out of bed and disappeared into the bathroom with an exaggerated pout. Probably looking for some mouthwash.

"If I knew who did it," the voice replied, "I wouldn't have said 'somebody.' Truth is, we're not sure who the new player is. But somebody has been shaking up the streets, kicking in doors, asking about our arrangement. Odds are this door-kicker is the one who hit Mason."

"Mason is a desk jockey who barely knows anything," the man said. "He was paid off to overlook some paperwork discrepancies, that's it. But the fact that our mysterious 'somebody' found out about him at all proves that people are talking a whole lot more than they should be and that pisses me off."

"Whoever this guy is, he must be a real scary son of a bitch to make people squeal on us."

"Then we need to be even scarier. Prove that we are not to be messed with. Time to send a message."

"You want Reardon's kid killed? Razor would be more than happy to cut his throat."

"Not yet. That kid is leverage. We kill his son, and Reardon's got nothing left to lose. But I want the players to know that flapping their gums has serious consequences."

"Hell, man, we just whacked Reardon's wife last night. She's not even in the ground yet. Think he's dumb enough to keep running his mouth?"

"I wouldn't think so," the man said, "but we'll send the message anyway, just to be sure. If it's him, maybe this will finally shut him up. If it's not him, maybe others will see what happens to him and think twice about crossing us."

"Want me to handle it?"

"No," the man said. "I'll have Omega take care of it. This is the kind of situation we pay him for."

"Omega? Your pet assassin? That man gives me the creeps. Something wrong with him."

"He's a highly-trained killing machine," the man replied. "Lethal to the extreme and probably borderline psychotic, if we're being honest. He's not supposed to sing you lullabies."

"You're the boss," the voice said and hung up.

The whore crawled back onto the bed, licking her lips with lascivious promise, but the man's lust had gone limper than a dead eel. He didn't even bother trying to coax it back to life. He threw a handful of cash at the girl and said, "Get lost. I've got some calls to make."

———

Lake George, New York

Omega sighted through the Armasight Drone Pro 10X Digital Night Vision rifle scope mounted on his M4 carbine and settled the cross-hairs on the scruffy tomcat stalking a three-legged rat. The whiskered rodent had pulled a chicken bone from a garbage bag and now perched on a cardboard box, oblivious to the cat sneaking in for the kill, just as the cat was oblivious to the gunman preparing to end his life. Prey and predator, locked in a savage cycle, with man at the top of the food chain.

As he thumbed the selector switch to single shot mode, Omega thought of his favorite quote, courtesy of Ernest Hemingway.

There is no hunting like the hunting of men, and those who have hunted armed men long enough and liked it, never care for anything else thereafter.

True story, no doubt about it. Nothing compared to the narcotic-like rush of running a man to the ground and spilling his blood... but killing cats was a close second. He despised the furry little bastards.

Cats were the assholes of the animal world. At least once a week, under cover of darkness, he would sneak into some randomly-chosen landfill with his NVS-equipped

M4. Rats came to eat the garbage, cats came to eat the rats, and Omega, in turn, hunted the cats, expressing his hatred with sound-suppressed 5.56mm bullets. It was a great stress reliever.

Technically he worked for a CIA black ops team under one of those ultra-covert programs that only a handful of high-ranking government officials knew about (and Omega seriously doubted even they knew the full extent of the dirty work the teams engaged in). Official classified documents showed Omega had been assigned two years ago to a DEA-CIA joint taskforce cobbled together to combat the influx of drugs entering the country by way of New York City's ports.

But in reality, that was all just a smokescreen designed to hide the truth. Because the truth was, he answered to just one man in the DEA and nothing he did helped stop the cocaine hemorrhaging into the city. Quite the opposite, in fact.

Bottom line, he was the hired muscle, the troubleshooter for the DEA bigshot pulling the strings on the alliance with the Colombian cartels.

The same DEA bigshot was now calling him on his cell phone. The ringtone was set to a Faster Pussycat song, his idea of a little joke.

He kept his eye locked to the scope as he pressed the encrypted phone to his ear. Eighty yards away, the cat crouched, tail twitching, evil eyes fixed on the rat. The rodent remained unaware that he was being hunted. Omega kept his voice low as he answered. "Yeah?" Through the scope, he watched as the rat's oversized incisors gnawed some gristle off the chicken bone.

"Where are you?" the man asked.

"Lake George."

"Isn't that up past Albany?"

"About an hour north."

"What are you doing way up there?"

"I suggest you don't ask questions you don't want answered," Omega replied.

"Are you shooting cats again, you sick freak?"

"We all have our hobbies."

"I need you back down here ASAP. I've got an assignment for you."

"Copy that. Name?"

"Reardon."

"I thought you had him under control," Omega said. "You snatched his kid and killed his wife, for god's sake."

"Apparently he's not getting the message yet," the man replied. "So you need to send him another one. Make it hurt."

"Just bury the brat and be done with it."

"You want to kill a kid?"

"Not my thing, but that Razor fella Sanchez has working for him is twisted enough to peel the skin off a baby."

"We kill his son, and we lose our only leverage to get that UC list."

Omega laughed softly and with just a hint of derision. "Yeah, because that's worked out so well for you. Cut off a couple of the boy's fingers, mail them to daddy in a box, and see how fast you get your list."

"Thanks for the advice," the man drawled sarcastically. "Now how about you let me handle the logistics of the situation, and you just do what I tell you. Last time I checked, that was the nature of our relationship."

"Got it. You're the boss." Omega hung up and just managed to get his finger back on the trigger as the tomcat pounced. He snap-fired, and the bullet caught the cat in midair. It hit the ground in a pile of bloody fur, thrashing like only a newly-dead cat can. Once the twitching subsided, the rat slithered in, gave it all a good sniff, and began to feast on the fresh feline meat.

Omega smirked as the rodent started chewing. Life can be savage, and sometimes the prey eats the predator. Too few people in this world understood that. He silently bid the rat happy eating and headed back to his vehicle. Killing cats was fun, but now it was time for some real blood-sport.

As Hemingway had said, nothing compared to hunting man.

———

Ten-year-old Jeremy Reardon was scared. Not a little scared like when he watched creepy movies—*really* scared.

He had no idea where he was. All he knew was that some very bad men were holding him prisoner. He didn't even know why, though he had overheard a couple of the kidnappers say it had to do with his father. Something about a list they wanted.

He'd been grabbed on his way home from school by a man he now knew was called Razor. They had put him on a plane, and even though he was afraid, the jet's vibrations had managed to lull him to sleep. He'd dreamed of going to the Great New York State Fair in Syracuse and eating cotton candy with his mom. The thump of the plane's wheels hitting the ground as it landed woke him up, his heartbeat starting to race again when he realized the dream was gone and he was still living in a nightmare.

Razor had shoved him into a Jeep and driven him deep into the jungle—even scared, Jeremy had looked for monkeys, but no luck—until they came to a large camp, or compound, as everyone had called it. Jeremy had been locked in this shed ever since. He was fed twice a day and taken to the outhouse to use the bathroom. It smelled really bad in there, but it wasn't like he had much choice. He used it as quickly as he could and got out of there.

Razor visited him in the shed every once in a while, but he usually didn't say much; just smiled and played with the big, shiny razor he carried. Jeremy guessed that was why they called him Razor because he couldn't imagine his parents had actually named him that. Then again, his own mom had almost named him Ichabod, so who knew what parents were thinking sometimes?

He heard footsteps outside his door and then the sound of someone sticking a key into the lock. A few seconds later Razor stepped into the shed and shut the door behind him. Jeremy's heart started beating fast, and he shivered a little bit.

"Hello, kid." Razor was dark-skinned and bald, with a soft, smooth voice that sounded dangerous at the same time. Jeremy was old enough to know that just because someone smiled and talked nicely didn't necessarily mean they were friendly. His father had once told him that just because a dog wagged its tail didn't mean it wouldn't bite you.

When Jeremy didn't respond to his greeting, Razor raised his straight-edge razor and let light from the overhead bulb gleam on the well-honed edge. It flashed into Jeremy's eyes like a silver starburst, making him squint. "What's the matter, kid? Cat got your tongue?"

Jeremy just stared at him. He was so scared that he felt like peeing his pants, but he tried not to let it show.

Razor chuckled. "You got *mucho cojones*, kid, you know that?" His hand suddenly shot out and grabbed Jeremy by the back of the neck. He pulled the boy close, thrust the razor between his legs, and snarled, "But next time I ask you a question, and you don't answer, I'll cut those *cojones* off and feed them to the dogs. You got that?"

Jeremy didn't know what kahonees were, but he was pretty sure he didn't want them cut off, so he said, "Yes, sir."

"You'd better." Razor shoved him away. "Unless you want to be a eunuch."

"I don't know what that means."

"Disrespect me again, and you'll find out." Razor turned to leave.

Jeremy blurted out, "What do you want with me, mister?"

Razor swung back around and fastened his reptilian eyes on the young boy. "It's nothing personal, kid. You're just insurance to make sure your daddy gives us what we need. Once he does that, you'll be on your way back home."

That sounded like a lie to Jeremy's ears, but he didn't say that out loud because he was afraid Razor would start chopping off his kahonees—whatever they were—if he did. Instead, he asked, "What happens if he doesn't give it to you?"

The devil's own black heart could not have been any colder than Razor's smile. "Then you're dead, kid." He mimicked a slashing motion across his throat and exited the shed in a burst of evil laughter.

———

Team Reaper Headquarters

Swift's fingers flew across the keyboard as he accessed the DEA's database, punching in the code to run the software program that would conceal his digital presence, cover his tracks, and scrub his virtual fingerprints. The DEA watchdogs would never even know he'd been in their system. Yeah, he probably could have Thurston call Jones and get him authorized access but going in the back door was more challenging. And therefore, more fun.

Swift was a bona fide keyboard warrior, and he wore that badge proudly. Sure, he could hit the field when called upon to do so, but he was no Reaper. Pretty much every other member of the team surpassed him at the run-and-gun stuff. But give him a computer, and he could set the world on fire. He had once boasted that he could hack the Pentagon using only a Commodore 64 with half the keys missing. That had been the last time he drank tequila.

He loved working for Team Reaper and remained grateful for the opportunity. The team accepted him as one of their own, respected him for his keyboard skills just as much as they respected Axe or Cara's ability to drill a bullseye from a thousand yards out. Nobody looked down on him as "just the computer geek." He'd suffered a bunch of sneers and ridicule over the course of his life, but he got none of that here.

With the scrubbing software activated, he typed in Steve Nash's name. Less than two seconds later, big red letters flashed across his monitor like neon beer signs in a barroom window, warning him that he did not possess the required security clearance to access the file.

"I've got your security clearance swinging right here," Swift muttered, fingers striking the keys with dizzying speed and extra force as if the flashing red letters were a personal affront. It took him less than a minute to sidestep the DEA's computerized cock-block and discover that Steve Nash worked for the DEA's Special Operations Division.

Given the secretive and controversial nature of the SOD—in addition to their tactical component, the SOD allegedly engaged in illegal wiretapping, unconstitutional searches, and evidence tampering in the everlasting war on drugs—it was no wonder the file was red-flagged.

Swift let out a low-and-slow whistle. It was starting to look like this alliance with the cartel—and the abduction of Jeremy Reardon—reached right into the upper ranks of the DEA. The thought left him with a cold feeling squirming through his guts like a clump of frozen maggots.

Intel on the Razor proved far easier to access, as it wasn't hidden behind any top-secret protocols. Heck, a rookie secretary in some Podunk field office could look at it if she wanted to.

The icy knot in the pit of his stomach expanded as he stared at the monitor and scrolled through the files. Razor was bad news any way you looked at it. A troubleshooter employed by the cartels, a coldblooded killer who liked to cut throats with his weapon of choice: a straight razor. According to the reports, Razor had a taste for torture, often skinning his victims alive and cutting them into pieces until they died, laughing as they screamed. The photos accompanying the reports were pure nightmare fuel, nothing but white bones gleaming through butchered meat. The DEA's most recent intel pegged the monster's location as somewhere in Colombia, currently working for Miguel Sanchez.

Swift studied the surveillance photo of the madman on the monitor. It had been taken through a top tier telescopic lens because the image was practically high-definition in clarity. Razor's eyes were those of a dead fish—cold and soulless and void of even a scintilla of emotion. The eyes of a psychopath who could peel the flesh from a sobbing child without his conscience so much as twitching. If he even had a conscience...

Swift could barely stomach the thought of this merciless killer being involved in the abduction of the Reardon boy. Thinking about Jeremy in Razor's torturous hands was enough to make him want to throw away his keyboard, gear up with all the full-auto firepower he could carry, and go monster-hunting. Instead, he gnawed worriedly at his lower lip as he sent all the intel to Reaper's phone. Right now it was Kane, Cara, and Axe's job to kick down doors, bust open heads, and kick bad guy butt. His job was to give them the information they needed to keep on ass-kicking.

And nobody kicked ass better than Reaper.

Swift called him back. "You should have everything you need on your phone," he said when Kane answered.

"Yeah, I got it. Thanks."

"Just note that Nash has a cabin on the Shawangunk Ridge near the Mohonk Preserve. Word is probably circulating by now that the players are being blitzed, so he may have bugged out. If he tucked tail and ran, that cabin is the obvious choice. Directions are in your intel packet."

"Copy that. Any luck on that other thing?"

"Not yet. I've got some analysis programs running in the background, sifting through what limited data is available so far, but nothing has pinged yet. I'll stay on it."

"Just as long as our mission remains primary."

"Always. Never doubt it."

"I never do," Kane replied. "Thanks again, Slick."

"Stay frosty out there."

Swift hung up and sat back in his chair, slumping a bit to rest his bones. He rubbed his bloodshot eyes to relieve them from the stress of staring at monitors for hours on end and silently wished his boots-on-the-ground teammates good luck. Hopefully, the gods of war would smile on them.

Because he would bet dollars to dimes that things were going to get a lot bloodier before they got better.

———

Reardon residence, New York

Mike Reardon sat in front of the television with a bottle of Jim Beam in one hand and the TV remote in the other, aimlessly flipping through the channels as he left sobriety in the rearview mirror. The bottle was half gone, and he was feeling no pain. Well, no *physical* pain. As for the emotional pain... there wasn't enough bourbon in the world to drown out the heartache he felt over the death of his wife.

He and Becky had just reconciled a little over a year ago. There'd been no affairs, no cheating; they had just sort of drifted apart and eventually separated over the usual "irreconcilable differences" people always cite when they can't pinpoint an exact reason. But it hadn't lasted long before they both realized they didn't want Jeremy to grow up in a split home. Becky had moved back in, and as the months progressed, they slowly but surely rekindled the romance they had lost somewhere along the way.

Now she was dead, the rekindled fire in her heart snuffed out by assassins' bullets. They'd already gotten hits on the gunmen's prints. Turned out they were low-level hitters for the cartels, streets rats with firepower, meaning his job had reached out and killed his wife. She was dead because of him.

He tilted his head back and dumped more alcohol down his throat. The bottle was almost empty, but he had another one ready to go. Tomorrow he had to meet with the funeral director to pick out a casket for Becky and no way on God's green earth he was doing that without a hangover. The booze burned going down, but he didn't care as long as it nudged him closer to unconsciousness. Right now passing out into a black, dreamless oblivion seemed like a sweet mercy.

He thought of Jeremy, alone, scared, completely unaware that he would never see his mother again. He refused to even consider the possibility that his son was dead too. He prayed to a God he was no longer sure existed and begged Him to keep his boy safe. He would do anything to save Jeremy, and he figured a little prayer couldn't hurt. With luck, Reaper and his team would bring his son home safe, but if not, a little divine intervention wouldn't be a bad backup plan. In Heckler & Koch, we trust, but God rides shotgun. Or something like that.

He kept hitting the bottle and staring at the TV, now stuck on some retro-channel playing one of those old sitcoms that would never get greenlit in today's PC culture. The more he drank, the more annoying the laugh-track became, grating on his ears. His wife dead, his son missing... what right did they have to laugh?

He drained the bottle down to its last dregs, then threw it at the television, shattering the screen. The annoying tinned-can laughter mercifully shut up.

He sensed the intruder behind him a split second before he caught the man's reflection in the fractured spider-web of the TV screen. He tried to spring up from the couch but was way too drunk for that, so instead he just sort of lumbered to his feet and turned to face the invader.

The man was dressed in black from head to toe with a balaclava masking his features. Reardon knew the mask was a "good" sign. No mask usually meant the person intended to leave no witnesses alive to identify them. Corpses point no fingers. This guy had clearly come for nefarious reasons —nobody breaks into a house wearing a balaclava to sell you Girl Scout cookies—but murder most likely wasn't on the menu tonight.

Reardon recognized the knife in the intruder's right hand as a Spyderco; the blade coated black to avoid reflecting light. He preferred Kershaw knives himself, but there was no denying the Spyderco was a quality piece. The man's left hand held a Heckler & Koch HK45 compact tactical pistol with a suppressor. He looked like something out of a video game or a B-grade action movie, standing there in all black with a gun in one hand and a knife in the other.

Reardon cursed himself for leaving his Glock in the bedroom. He was a damn fool, and even his booze-soaked brain knew it. He'd been too worried about drowning his sorrows in Jim Beam, forgetting the old adage that pain is a champion swimmer. Now it looked like he might pay a steep price for the tactical error.

Of course, if he could make it to the kitchen, there was a wooden block full of knives—everything from little paring knives to thick-bladed meat cleavers—sitting on the counter. Not as good as his Glock but better than nothing.

As if reading his mind, the intruder moved to cut off his access to the kitchen. "Not gonna happen, Mikey. Settle down and let's get this over with."

"Who are you?" Reardon demanded though the slurred speech dulled some of the toughness. "What do you want?"

"You can call me Omega," the masked man said. "And what I want is to deliver a message."

"I'm all ears."

"Afraid it's not that kind of message, Mike."

"You work for the cartels?"

Omega just stared at him, not responding.

"You know where my son is, you piece of shit?"

"I'm not here to answer your fucking questions, Mike. I'm here to cut you down to size." Omega raised the HK and smacked a bullet into Reardon's kneecap.

While undercover in a biker gang that had been running heroin along the Texas/Mexico border, Reardon had once had his testicles plucked by a sadistic senorita, beaten like a pair of punching bags, and then squeezed in a pair of rusty vice-grips. But all that pain paled in comparison to the abrupt agony of his knee shattering like hammered ice when the bullet hit home.

He immediately corkscrewed to the floor, banging his ribs off the coffee table before landing on his back. The empty liquor bottle lay near his head from where it had ricocheted off the TV and bounced onto the floor. Through the pain that threatened to black him out, he had the thought that the bottle might make a good weapon. Well, maybe not *good*, but better than nothing.

But before he could even start to reach for it, Omega hurdled the couch and closed on him in an instant, knife a black-steeled blur, and Reardon descended into a slicing, slashing hell.

As the blade carved open his flesh, Reardon tried to fight him off, but it was useless. He was a kitten trying to fend off a grizzly bear. Omega was clearly a tier-one operator; drunk and crippled, Reardon didn't stand a chance.

He raised his arms to block the Spyderco's stabs and slashes but only succeeded in getting them cut up too. Omega was careful not to kill him, but the assassin opened dozens of wounds in nonlethal sections of Reardon's frame.

Some were skin-shallow cuts, some were tissue-deep tears, and others bit in all the way down to the bone. Blood flowed freely, staining the carpet.

As Omega sliced a trench down Reardon's lower jaw from ear to chin, he growled, "Here's the message, Mikey—call off your fucking dogs."

Reardon didn't even try to reply. The room spun and blurred, his eyes hazed with crimson from all the blood spattered on his face. He just laid there, enveloped in a cocoon of pain from which he knew he would not metamorphose into a beautifully scarred butterfly, but a broken, beat-down bug.

Omega placed the tip of the knife a hairsbreadth from the DEA agent's left eye. "You hearing me, Mikey? I need some kind of acknowledgment. Or do I need to take one of your eyes to make my point?"

"I hear you," Reardon managed to croak when he really wanted to scream. There was only so much suffering a man could endure before breaking, and he could feel the threads of sanity snapping like razor-kissed rubber bands.

Omega kept the knife-point nearly pricking Reardon's eye, and for a couple of heart-stopping seconds, he thought the assassin was really going to plunge the blade through his pupil like a grill skewer impaling a cherry tomato. But then Omega wiped the Spyderco on the shredded remnants of Reardon's shirt, deftly folded the knife one-handed, and tucked it away. Now you see it, now you don't, please enjoy your lacerations.

He reached up with a gloved hand and patted Reardon on his slashed cheek like you would pat a well-behaved dog on the head. "That's a good boy, Mikey. Don't make me come back here or I'll paint the walls with your blood."

Rockland County, New York

Kane, Cara, and Axe studied Swift's intel as they chowed down on dubious egg salad sandwiches that looked like they *might* have been fresh somewhere in the last three days and lukewarm fountain cola from an all-night gas station on the Rockland County line. As body-fuel went, it beat going hungry, but Kane hoped he didn't get a gut-ache during the back end of the blitz.

"At this stage of the game, it's a longshot that Nash is still lying low at home," Axe opined. "I agree with what Slick said. If this guy is SOD, then he's no fool, so he must have bugged out by now, and that cabin is the logical choice."

"Still a gamble," Kane replied. "For all we know, Nash could be running for the border."

"Can only hit the targets we have and hope Lady Luck is riding with us," Axe countered.

"Too bad she's such a fickle bitch," Kane said. "But you're right. Right now, the cabin is our only play."

"Somebody should still check his house," Cara suggested. "Cover all the bases."

Kane nodded. "Time to split up. Axe, Cara, you two head for the cabin. I'll recon the house. I should reach my target first, so if he's not there, I'll give you a heads up."

They both nodded in acknowledgment.

Kane's phone rang. Looking at the number, he said, "It's Traynor."

Axe muttered, "That's not a good sign."

Kane answered, cutting right to the chase. "If you're calling me, something went sideways."

"That's an understatement," Traynor replied.

"What happened?"

"Somebody hit Mike Reardon right in his damn house, that's what happened." The anger came through loud and clear in Traynor's tone. "He'll live, but he's hurt pretty bad, Reaper. They shot out one of his knees and cut him all up. Brick and I are heading over there now. Arenas is staying with the plane."

"Can Reardon ID the attacker?"

"Negative. The hitter wore a mask. Called himself Omega. Told Mike to call off his dogs."

"Yeah, well, he's got a better chance of face-fucking a rattlesnake and not getting bit. You go take care of your buddy. We're moving on to the next phase of the blitz. The sooner we take these bastards down, the sooner Reardon will be safe."

"Roger that, Reaper. Give us a shout if you need anything."

"The only thing we'll be needing pretty soon is body bags," Kane said grimly.

———

Reardon residence

When Traynor and Brick arrived at Reardon's house, they found the DEA agent lying on the floor in a blood-splattered mess. Brick got right to work. For a big man—6'3" in his bare feet—the former Navy SEAL, now Team Reaper combat medic, was surprisingly gentle while tending to the wounds.

"I could probably stitch up most of those lacerations," he announced. "But no matter what, he's gonna have to go to a hospital for that knee."

"I'm right here," Reardon said, voice weak from shock and blood loss. "Don't talk around me."

"Right. Sorry." Brick looked him right in the eye. "The bullet hit dead center on your patella, or kneecap, as it's more commonly called. Nothing but shattered bone and torn up tendons. I'm good, but I'm not *that* good. You need a surgeon and some top shelf painkillers."

"And not the kind named Jim Beam," Traynor added.

"Will they be able to fix it?" Reardon asked, grimacing. "Give it to me straight."

"I don't see why not. Probably looking at a full knee replacement and you'll most likely always have a limp, but you'll live."

Traynor called for an ambulance. When he hung up with the dispatcher, Reardon gave him one of the most miserable looks he had ever seen on a human face. "Pete," the DEA agent croaked hoarsely, "maybe we should call it off. Tell Reaper to stand down."

"That's crap talk, Mike, and I think you know it," Traynor replied.

"Crap? For god's sake, Pete, look at me. Whoever these people are, they sent someone to my house to carve me up like a damn turkey. What if they do something like this to Jeremy? I could never live with myself."

"They hurt you, Mike. No doubt about it. Hurt you bad." Traynor paused. "But they didn't kill you. They let you live because they still want something from you, and that's the same reason you gotta believe your boy is still safe."

"Yeah, they want something," Reardon echoed. "Something I don't have. Something I can't give them. Something that doesn't even exist."

"They don't know that," Traynor reminded him.

"Pete, I'm begging you, call off the blitz. You're going to get Jeremy killed." Tears spilled from the corners of his eyes, cutting clean tracks through all the blood. "I never should have called you."

Traynor recognized the tone of voice, somewhere between dull and desperate. His buddy was broken, his soul crushed, his cross of suffering too heavy to bear. Hard to blame him. Son missing, wife dead, kneecapped, slashed to hell... right now, Reardon was a modern-day version of Job and God was dumping all sorts of tribulations down on his head. That kind of bad shit would shake any man's faith.

"I get where you're coming from," Traynor said. "Honestly, man, I do. But you did call us, and you can't un-ring that war bell, buddy. We've got three damn good people, the best of the best, out there ghosting through the night to run down the scumbags behind all this shit. Reaper will storm the gates of hell if that's what it takes to bring your boy back. But one thing he will *not* do is turn his back and ignore a DEA-cartel alliance. That's too big to walk away from, and you know it."

Traynor believed every word he said. Nothing would pull Reaper off the hunt. He and Brick would get Reardon to a hospital and get him patched up; meanwhile, Kane would continue to tear apart this corrupt alliance piece by dirty piece. Those who had kidnapped Jeremy Reardon would pay. Those who had ordered Becky Reardon murdered would pay. And those who had viciously attacked Mike Reardon would pay.

Pay in blood, damn straight.

What had happened here tonight was terrible, but it would not make Reaper hit the brakes, not by a long shot. If anything, it would steel their resolve. They were a covert fast-reaction team, emphasis on the word *fast*. Leave the bureaucratic bullshit and handwringing for someone else. Team Reaper hit the ground running, and they didn't slow down until they completed the mission or died trying.

Sirens sounded in the distance, their droning wail piercing the night.

"Here comes your ride," Brick said to Reardon.

"Maybe I'll get lucky and die on the way," Reardon mumbled.

Traynor pointed a firm finger at him. "You cancel that crap right now, brother. I know you're in a lot of pain, inside and out, but don't you dare talk like that."

"Sorry, Pete. It's just..." More tears spilled.

Traynor softened his voice. "Yeah, man, I know."

He ached for his hurting buddy and wished he could take away his pain. Mike Reardon had been a bona fide badass back in the day, but now he just looked—and sounded—weak and broken, a man from whom all zest for life had been stolen. His will to live had been sucked right out of him, leaving behind a hollow shell. Traynor reckoned that if they failed to save Jeremy, Reardon would probably end up gargling a gun barrel.

"Swear to me," the DEA agent said. "Swear to God that you're going to bring my boy home."

Even now, when a fake promise might have brought comfort, Traynor refused to lie to his friend. Instead, he gave him the truth. "I swear to God we're gonna try."

"He's all I got left, Pete."

"I know."

"You find him, Pete. You find him, and then you rip the guts right out of whoever took him from me."

"Reaper is hitting the next target as we speak."

Reardon looked at him with haunted eyes as the ambulance crew rushed in. "Whoever it is, if they had anything to do with this, you make him hurt. Make him hurt *bad*."

"If he can lead us to your boy, then Kane will make him scream like hell if that's what it takes."

CHAPTER 5

Shawangunk Ridge, New York

Steve Nash's nerves jangled, but he was too seasoned an operator to get seriously rattled. Panic was for sissies. Sure, he felt fear, but he put a choke collar on that mutt and used the fear to fuel his survival instincts. Controlled fear kept you sharp, helped you maintain your edge, and true warriors knew how to channel it to their needs. The adrenalin pumped hot through his veins, setting his blood on fire, triggered by the alarming phone call he received earlier.

"Hello?"

"You're being hunted. Code Blue."

The words came out in one long, run-on rush. Then, with a click, the line went dead.

Code Blue, the signal for evasive action. Basically, he had been advised to blow town and lay low until the heat simmered down. It left a bad taste in his mouth—he preferred fight to flight—but he knew his bosses expected him to suck it up, swallow it down, and obey their orders.

He grabbed his bugout bag and hopped in his Dodge

Charger. As he whipped out into the street, the weight of the Colt .45 riding in shoulder leather gave him comfort. He was a big believer in .45s over 9mms or .40s or—God forbid—.38s. The bigger a hole you could blow in somebody, the better.

A grim smile ghosted his lips as he punched the gas and smoked some rubber off the tires. If these mysterious operators wanted to tangle with Steve Nash, then he would be more than happy to make them eat their own guts. They could try to play tough while slurping on their own innards. He had plenty of combat experience, and no Rambo wannabes would have him pissing his pants.

If not for the Code Blue command, Nash would have hung around to test his mettle against these motherless pricks. But where the Colombian cartels were concerned, you followed orders, or you found your tongue yanked out through your esophagus in a gruesome parody of a necktie.

So he would get out of the city and hole up in his lodge until the storm passed. Maybe hunt some deer over on the Mohonk Preserve tomorrow, fry up some tenderloins for supper. Sure, they weren't in season, but when you're one of the top dogs in the DEA assisting the cartels with smuggling tons of cocaine into the United States—and getting filthy rich in the process, thanks to some carefully-laundered funds in offshore accounts—a little poaching just didn't seem like that big of a deal.

Nash parked his Charger at the base of the private drive leading up to his cabin. The rest of the way was too rugged for the sports car. He fetched a four-wheeler from a small shed under a nearby tree, oblivious to the fact that his head was divided into four quadrants by the crosshairs of a sniper's scope.

"Need me to range you?" Cara asked, straight-faced but her tone sarcastic, keeping her voice *sotto voce* so it wouldn't carry on the night air as she lay prone in the dirt and leaves beside Axe. The ex-recon marine sniper had the M110A1 CSASS tucked tight in his shoulder pocket, eye behind the scope.

With the crosshairs aligned on his target, Axe didn't want to move his head and lose the sight picture, so he tried to inject some glare into his voice as he growled, "It's under two hundred meters. I could make this shot with my eyes closed."

Cara smiled. "Just offering."

"Shut up and let me shoot this guy."

Kane had sent word that Nash had bugged out. They had set up an ambush on the wooded slope that rose above the southern side of the cabin's private drive. They had been lying in wait for the last two hours. In another ninety minutes, it would be dawn, but right now the moon still ruled the sky.

"Don't kill him," Cara reminded. "We need him alive."

"Yeah, I got it." Through the scope, Axe watched Nash fire up the four-wheeler's engine. It rumbled to life, and after giving it a few revs, he headed up the trail, dirt spraying from beneath the knobby tires.

Axe made a slight adjustment to the cross-hairs. His finger took up trigger slack to the breakpoint.

The four-wheeler's headlights flicked on at the same time Axe sent a bullet tearing through the darkness.

Nash yelled in pain as the high-velocity impact smashed him off the ATV, his left shoulder exploding at the joint, leaving his arm dangling by just a few mangled threads. He smacked down in the dirt, the gravel gouging ruts from his face.

"Not sure if he's got a gun or not, but he's definitely not well-armed," Axe deadpanned.

Cara groaned. "Sniper jokes are worse than dad jokes."

Nash was clearly smart enough to realize his attackers were still out there, waiting, lurking, concealed by the night. He knew he needed cover and needed it quick. He began dragging himself toward the four-wheeler, which had veered off the trail and stopped against a tree once it lost its rider but was still running.

Before their quarry could reach the ATV, Axe drilled two rounds into the fuel tank, turning it into a fireball. Chunks of burning wreckage rose into the air and then fell back to earth like a rain shower from hell. Axe saw a piece of molten rubber spatter Nash's face and cling there like napalm, eating through the flesh. He clawed at it with his good hand as he climbed to his feet and stumbled toward the woods, no doubt looking for somewhere to hide.

"He's running," Cara said.

"Not for long." Axe sent another shot thundering through the darkness.

The bullet nailed Nash in the back of his left knee and damn near blew his lower leg off. He howled in agony and crashed to the ground, clutching at the blood-spurting injury.

With their target down and not going anywhere, Axe and Cara vacated their sniper's nest and made their way down the slope, threading through the rocks and trees until they materialized out of the shadows, standing in a silvery slash of moonlight.

They stared down at Nash with eyes chiseled from arctic ice. Not the cold, soulless emotion of a shark, but the cold determination to do whatever it took, without hesitation, to get the job done. With their ice-eyed gazes, they let Nash know that there would be no mercy, no backing down. Time was ticking, and they had come to play rough.

With a kid's life on the line, and as a mother herself, Cara knew she would go to any extreme necessary to get Jeremy Reardon back. Crossing lines, breaking rules, getting her hands bloody... sometimes that was the only play left.

But clearly Nash wasn't one to just crap his pants, roll over, and fold like a paper tiger. With his system no doubt jacked up to red zone levels on pain, he nevertheless snarled, "Fuck you."

Axe responded by crashing a boot into Nash's mouth. Teeth shot everywhere like broken Scrabble tiles. The blow sent him sprawling flat on his back as blood continued to pour from his knee and shoulder, forming a sticky puddle that looked black in the moonlight.

"Watch your mouth," Axe growled. "I don't think your mother would approve of that kind of language."

"Go to hell," Nash spat.

Cara drew her Sig M17 and held it muzzle-down by her leg. "Stop talking and start listening. The DEA has become bed buddies with the cartels. Word on the street is you know who the top dogs are. We want their names."

"Eat shit," Nash hissed through pain-clenched teeth.

"Buckle up, boy-o," Cara said. "It's about to get rough."

Axe kicked him in the face again. Two more teeth sluiced down his throat on a river of blood. He choked and gagged and vomited up chunks of shattered enamel.

"If I wanted to eat shit," Axe said, "I'd go to your mother's house for supper."

Cara knew plenty of operators who disavowed torture, calling it an immoral waste of time, but that was crap.

When you needed someone to give up information fast, the escalation of pain would usually get the job done. Those who made up excuses about the ineffectiveness of torture for intelligence-gathering were just afraid of their actions being labeled barbaric.

Cara didn't care if they called her barbaric or not. Nash was a bad guy, and she would torture the shit out of a bad guy to save an innocent boy.

She crouched down and jammed the Sig's muzzle into Nash's lower abdomen, right between nuts and navel. "Give me the names, or I'll blow your guts out."

Pain, shock, and blood loss conspired to send Nash drifting into a numbing Neverland. But he snapped out of it when Cara stabbed even deeper with the pistol barrel.

"I don't know!" he yelled, blood spraying like spittle from his crushed lips. "You hear me, bitch? I don't know!"

Cara took no pleasure in torture, but when the time came, she didn't hesitate. Especially when the subject was a corrupt DEA agent who helped the cartels flood the country with cocaine, murder an innocent woman, and kidnap a little boy.

The Sig bucked once, the report muffled by the muzzle's point-blank proximity to Nash's stomach. His entire body convulsed as the bullet blasted all the way through. Blood sprayed across the ground, and Cara knew the scavengers would soon come sniffing around.

"Warned you," she said. "Now give me the names. I've got fourteen more bullets in this thing right now, plus three backup mags. I will make your life unbelievably miserable."

Nash was clearly broken. No more foul curses or profane insults out of his mouth, just groans of agony. He had probably been trained in torture-endurance techniques, but that only got you so far. The human body can only take so much suffering before mental willpower cracks. Nash had been put through the wringer by a couple of warriors who would smile at the devil right before they shot him in the balls. With one arm and one leg blown off and a slow-kill gut-shot giving him a drawn-out, agonizing death, all he wanted now was an end to the pain. He would have sold his mother for a mercy bullet to the head, and the puppet-masters behind the DEA-cartel alliance were damn sure not his mother.

As the hurt crashed through his body in waves, his mouth fired information like a machinegun. Cara and Axe listened intently as he laid out the whole dirty operation, including the names of the head honchos.

Paul Jacobs and Miguel Sanchez.

The men behind the curtain. The string-pullers. The dirtbags at the top.

Otherwise known as dead men walking, as far as Team Reaper was concerned.

"What about Jeremy Reardon?" Cara asked. "Where's he being held?"

"I don't know," Nash said.

Cara rapped the Sig against his remaining kneecap. "Do not lie to me, Nash."

"I don't know!" he said, louder this time. "Shoot me again if that's what you gotta do, but I don't know where the damn kid is!"

"You'd better tell me how to find him before I get all trigger happy again."

"Jacobs," Nash blurted. "Jacobs will know where he is."

Cara nodded. It had the ring of truth to it, plus it made sense. "Fair enough," she said, removing the gun from his knee.

Nash looked up at her. "Now kill me already, will ya?"

"Sure." Cara raised the Sig and shot him between the eyes, blowing his brains out the back of his skull and ending his misery.

"You okay?" Axe asked.

"I'm fine," she replied. "He had it coming."

"You're damn right he did."

"Let's get out of here."

They didn't waste any time looking at Nash. They had killed him, he was dead, and that was that. They'd seen plenty of guys with their heads blown off. Axe canted the rifle over his shoulder as they walked away, and Cara holstered her pistol. They had blitzed their way up the ranks and now had the top dogs in their sights. The dealers of white death were collapsing one by one, the dominos falling, the illicit empire starting to crumble. The savages were getting savaged. But Team Reaper's work wasn't done. Not by a long shot.

Jeremy Reardon wasn't home yet.

Until he was, the blood and thunder would continue.

CHAPTER 6

Cathedral Church of Saint John the Divine Manhattan, New York

The Cathedral Church of Saint John the Divine, in Manhattan, could claim to be the fifth largest Christian church in the world, a stunning architectural masterpiece of stone-on-stone construction in the Gothic Revival design that boasted the largest Rose window in the United States. Tourists and parishioners alike often commented that the church was so breathtakingly beautiful, it felt like holiness permeated the place, the stones infused with the hundreds of thousands of prayers that had been uttered in hushed, reverent tones over the centuries.

The Right Reverend Christopher Wilkes wondered if perhaps a hundred thousand prayers were sailing heaven-ward right at this very moment as he looked out at the sea of troubled faces. For better or worse, many people turned to God, however temporarily, after a tragedy. Wilkes hadn't seen a crowd of this size gathered since the morning after the Twin Towers fell. Now, the morning after yesterday's trio of terrorist attacks on the city, the cathedral's hallowed walls once again swelled with hurting souls seeking answers, seeking hope, seeking solace.

What they got instead were death and destruction.

As the organ notes faded, Reverend Wilkes began a solemn speech, his tone warm and comforting. "Brothers and sisters, yesterday was perhaps the darkest day we have ever seen, but today is a new day, and with a new day comes new hope. Hope that light will emerge from the darkness and—"

His last words. The bomb blast cut off the rest. The Right Reverend Wilkes was blown to pieces, along with everyone in the front three rows. They had come hoping to hear from God; in the blink of an eye, they all met Him.

Three more explosions rocked the sanctuary, filling the holy place with fire and debris. Blood and body parts flew through the air like broken toys flung by an angry child. The dead lay twisted and mangled while the dying screamed and writhed in their final moments. The wounded crawled toward the door, dragging themselves across the floor, weeping eyes fixed on their salvation. Many were trampled underfoot by the panicked survivors stampeding for the exit; the breath smashed from their lungs.

In the final tally, the bombing of the Cathedral Church of Saint John the Divine left one hundred and twenty-three dead and nearly double that wounded.

They had come seeking Heaven.

They found hell instead.

––––––––

George Washington Bridge (GWB)
New York / New Jersey

The GWB connecting New Jersey and Manhattan is considered the busiest bridge in the world, and while the morning after the three terrorist attacks saw a noticeable decrease in traffic as people avoided the city, it was still congested on the iconic double-deck suspension bridge during the morning commute. Not bumper to bumper like usual, but the bridge was still busy.

However, the congestion proved no problem for the eighteen-wheeler oil tanker truck that rammed its way through the traffic, smashing cars out of its way as it plowed right up the middle of the four lanes, leaving crushed metal and broken glass in its wake. It was a live-action version of demolition derby, cars spinning away from the bruising contact of the big rig, sparks flying as steel grated against steel. Drivers who saw the truck coming tried to get out of the way, but there was nowhere to go, no room to maneuver out of the path of destruction.

Smaller cars were shoved on top of other vehicles, collapsing the roofs and trapping—sometimes killing—the occupants within. Electric sparks hissed across spilled fuel pouring from broken lines and set cars ablaze. It took just under ninety seconds for the eighteen-wheeler to brutally force its way to the center of the bridge, the midway point between the two gigantic suspension towers. It then jack-knifed to the left, skidding the oil tanker across all four lanes. It rammed another car in the process, flipping it onto its roof.

When the semi-truck shuddered to a stop, the door popped open, and the driver emerged. Wearing an olive drab balaclava, thin leather gloves, and a yellow running suit, he clambered up on top of the tanker as a symphony of curses, screams, and honking horns goaded him on.

He turned and faced the destruction he had caused,

surveying the wreckage strewn behind him after his maniacal charge to the center of the bridge. Nobody could see it, but beneath the mask, he smiled. He raised his arms like a Pentecostal preacher about to pray down revival and shouted, "*Allahu Akbar!* Bin Laden rises!"

At that moment, the people closest to the jackknifed rig noticed the detonator in the man's right fist. Small, unobtrusive, and oh so deadly. It was the last thing they saw before they were vaporized.

The liquid explosive that filled the tanker instead of oil detonated with a massive, devastating blast that blew the bridge right in half, shearing through the steel and concrete of the upper and lower decks like they were made of balsa wood. Severed suspension cables snapped through the air like razored whips, slicing apart anyone unlucky enough to be in their path.

Without support, the bridge collapsed. The explosion sent punishing shock waves rippling outward, tearing apart the road. Hundreds of vehicles plunged two hundred feet into the murky waters of the Hudson River. Many people were killed on impact. Scores of others drowned, trapped underwater in their cars while their luck—and breath—ran out. Huge chunks of debris crashed down on others like meteorites, crushing them into oblivion. Those that survived the initial plunge into the Hudson were often killed moments later as more cars fell on top of them.

The attack had been carefully planned for maximum carnage.

It had succeeded.

It would take days to count the dead.

The White House

President Carter had just finished his breakfast when news of the bombing at the Cathedral Church of Saint John the Divine came in, followed less than thirty minutes later by the horrific attack on the George Washington Bridge.

My God, he thought. *Not again.* He felt ill, his stomach churning with sour acid as he stared at the terrible images on the television screen. The main picture showed the collapsed bridge. A smaller insert in the lower right corner of the screen showed the church, black smoke curling from its shattered windows and rising heavenward as if to touch God's feet and ask Him why He had allowed this to happen.

He had invited Hank Jones and Kevin McNanes to join him for breakfast, requesting personal updates on various missions the men were overseeing. Now all three of them just stared at the mass destruction on the TV. It seemed almost impossible that they had been hit again, but there it was in living color. The President wondered how much more New York City could take. For that matter, how much more could *America* take? Terrorism had come to the country's shores once again, on a scale rarely seen or imagined.

McNanes, the National Security Advisor, summed up what they were all thinking. "I guess that bastard wasn't bluffing about hitting us with more attacks today."

"I wonder who's funding them," Jones said. "Most terrorist organizations, even the headline grabbers like ISIS and Al-Qaeda, aren't exactly rolling in money. Yet somehow they've managed to acquire a plane, boats, Semtex, a missile launcher, a tractor-trailer, and whatever the hell kind of explosive was in that tanker. Seems to me either somebody won a few million on a scratch-off ticket or this cell found themselves a sugar daddy to bankroll their holy war."

"You know what I wonder?" President Carter said. "I wonder what we're going to do to stop more attacks from happening. Answer me that, gentlemen."

"The martial law option is still on the table," Jones replied. "Put NYC on lockdown."

"That'll play well on the campaign trail," Carter muttered. "Just about guarantee I don't get elected for a second term."

Jones arched an eyebrow. "Never knew you to make a decision based on political maneuvering," the Chairman of the Joint Chiefs said. He kept his tone respectful even though his words held a subtle rebuke.

"I don't make decisions based solely on the political ramifications," Carter replied. "But only a fool doesn't look at all the angles."

"You could spin it," Jones suggested. "Point out that you'll do whatever it takes to keep America safe, conse-quences be damned. Feed that talking point to some of our key friends in the press and let it get some media play."

"That's not how the other side will spin it. They'll just point out that on my watch, America suffered one of its worst terrorist attacks in history. They'll say my intelligence agencies were incompetent, or underfunded, or that I ignored critical information. And if I declare martial law in New York and, God forbid, more attacks occur, they'll accuse me of incompetence and demand I step down, if they don't try to outright impeach me."

"Even if any of that were true—and it's not," Jones said, "none of it is impeachable."

Carter snorted. "Like they care about that."

"They can say whatever they want," McNanes bristled,

"but our intelligence agencies are not incompetent."

President Carter gave him a frank stare. "We have been hit by five terrorist attacks in twenty-four hours. I'm not pointing any fingers or saying incompetence is to blame here, but we definitely missed something, and let's not pretend otherwise."

McNanes nodded. "Of course, Mr. President." His phone buzzed. He glanced at the number, then looked at Carter and Jones. "Excuse me, I should take this."

He was on the phone less than a minute before hanging up. "That was our heads-up," he informed them. "The networks have a new tape from Johnny Jihad. They're going live with it in three minutes."

"Wonderful," Carter growled. "I'm just giddy with anticipation."

A few minutes later, the reporter announced they had breaking news, and they rolled the tape. Johnny Jihad, still hooded and masked, spoke again in front of the shredded, blood-splattered American flag.

"You were warned that we would strike again," the terrorist proclaimed. "Al-Qaeda has risen, the spirit of Bin Laden has risen, and your infidel nation has once again suffered fire and fury for its unholy crimes against Allah. You have defied the will of the one true God, refused to obey the sacred scriptures, and great death has been your bloody reward. More death will follow soon, unless your President, Jack Carter, surrenders himself to me for execution."

"There it is again," Carter muttered. "At least we know what the son of a bitch wants."

"People always want what they can't have," Jones remarked.

"America will continue to suffer the slaughter until your

President is dead. Your nation claims to be a Christian nation, a faith based on the sacrifice of one man. Well, now one man can once again sacrifice himself to save the lives of millions. When President Carter is burning in Hell for the crimes he has committed against the Islamic people, only then will my jihad cease."

"Crimes? What crimes? What is this guy even talking about?" McNanes snapped. "We haven't even messed with Al-Qaeda much in recent years. They weren't seen as a viable threat after we kicked their sorry asses halfway back to the Stone Age."

"Or so you thought," Carter commented.

McNane's face reddened at the reminder that somehow, some way, they had dropped the ball.

"I'm sure it's just the usual rhetoric," Jones said. "Complaining about our military activity in the Middle East or whining about our alliance with Israel. We've heard it all before. The only new twist is the demand for the President's death."

"Maybe it's personal," Carter said. "The guy clearly wants me in a body bag."

Jones grunted, "I know some people right here in Congress that want that."

"Ain't that the truth."

On the TV, Johnny was outlining his demands. "At sunset today, President Carter will take a boat here." He held up a piece of paper with nautical coordinates written on it.

Jones scanned the numbers. "That's about fifteen miles out from Long Island."

"If necessary, he may be accompanied by one person to pilot the boat. Once President Carter is in my possession, the pilot will be released unharmed."

The terrorist leaned in close to the camera, near enough for them all to see the fanatical fires blazing in his eyes. "The President will be swiftly beheaded, his death screams recorded, and the video broadcast for all the world to see. Then, and only then, will the attacks on America cease. If you do not comply, another massacre will take place tomorrow." Johnny paused, moving in even closer to the camera, before concluding, "Is the life of one man worth the lives of many? That is the choice that America, the New Babylon, must now make."

The screen cut to black. The news reporter returned and began summoning various experts to analyze the terrorist's demands.

President Carter grabbed the remote and hit the Mute button to silence the media circus, then sighed wearily. "Well, that's just frigging fantastic."

"Could be a bluff," McNanes said. "It's very possible, even likely, that he exhausted his resources pulling off the attacks yesterday and today. Threatening another attack tomorrow isn't the same as being able to actually make it happen."

"We thought that yesterday," the President reminded him, "and today we have a bombed church and a collapsed bridge. At this point, I think it's best we stop underestimating this madman's capabilities."

"Agreed," said Jones. "Moving forward, we have to assume they are capable of carrying out any threats they make."

"So what's the plan?" Carter gestured at the muted television. "He's made his demands, and now the clock is ticking. What's our best course of action?"

"I have an idea," Jones said. "But I'm not sure you're going to like it."

"Let's hear it."

"We give him what he wants."

"Are you crazy?" McNanes exploded. "You want to hand the President over to be butchered?"

"In a manner of speaking."

Carter arched an eyebrow. "Ballsy play," he said to Jones. "Especially when it's not your balls on the chopping block."

"Of course I don't mean we serve you up on a platter with an apple in your mouth, ready for the slaughter," Jones clarified. "We use a decoy."

"What do you mean by 'decoy'?" McNanes asked.

Jones gave him a look. "I think you know exactly what I mean."

The President said, "You want to send someone in my place."

"That's insane." McNanes shook his head. "You can't be serious."

"It's not insane, and I'm dead serious," Jones replied. "This is our best shot at luring these rats out from whatever hole they're hiding in." He pointed at Carter. "They want the President, and they've told us where they'll pick him up. We make them think we're complying and then when they come to make the pickup, we grab them."

"How do you plan on making the grab?" McNanes asked. "The drop-off coordinates are in the middle of the ocean, remember? They'll see any backup team from miles away."

"Simple," Jones replied. "We use SDVs, or a mini-sub if one's available, to insert a SEAL team beneath the boat. These Al-Qaeda clowns will never know what hit 'em."

"I like the way you think," Carter said.

McNanes wasn't convinced. "What if our boy Johnny

doesn't show up for the grab? He could just send some subordinates. Then he'll know we screwed him over and he'll launch another attack."

"That's a possibility," Jones admitted. "But if we just sit around twiddling our thumbs, the attack happens anyway. I'd rather do something to try to prevent the attack from happening than just sit back, do nothing, and hope for the best."

President Carter said, "Hank makes a good point. I prefer action to inaction, even when it comes with some risk."

"Plus," Jones added, "even if we don't nail Johnny, we can hopefully take one of his errand boys alive and ask them some hard questions about his whereabouts."

"Hard questions," McNanes echoed with a frown. "You mean torture."

"I believe the politically correct term is 'enhanced inter-rogation,'" Jones said. "But yeah, we turn the screws until they give up their boss."

"Dirty business," McNanes muttered. "I shouldn't even be hearing this."

Jones shrugged. "Then leave the room. No shame in being squeamish. But make no mistake, I will do whatever is necessary to protect American lives."

President Carter waved away the discussion. "Save the moral debate for later. Right now, we need to execute this plan."

"Getting the SEAL team into place will be easy enough," Jones replied. "I'll call Chief Hunt and make that happen ASAP."

"Who's going to be the decoy?" McNanes asked.

"I've got someone in mind," Jones said. "And he's already in New York."

CHAPTER 7

The Sanchez compound
Colombia

Razor stood in the middle of the warehouse and gazed upon the seemingly endless supply of neatly-packaged powder. "White Death" the anti-drug coalitions called it, but to the junkies addicted to the narcotic rush, it was more like White Bliss. Razor never touched the stuff, but he had heard it described as snorting heaven up your nose.

Thanks to reduced media coverage, people believed cocaine usage had declined since the 1980s, but it was actually more popular than ever, just not as mainstream as it had been during the Reagan area—meth and heroin had stolen the spotlight.

Razor found it amusing that the country that kick-started the so-called "War on Drugs" had the world's worst drug problem. Illicit narcotics flowed into the United States like a plague. A plague that Americans were paying billions of dollars for. A plague that was making the drug cartels wealthier than King Solomon. The cartels could burn thousand dollar bills with the same lack of concern most men feel when they lose a penny.

Razor stepped out of the warehouse and gazed across the clearing at the laboratory. The chemists were there now, cooking up more poison to sell to the Americans. With the DEA's own Special Operations Division protecting the US portion of the pipeline and all the right people paid to turn a blind eye, Razor had little doubt that the next shipment would reach the shores of America without incident. It was a perfect partnership, one that ensured continued success and accumulation of wealth.

A voice interrupted his thoughts. "Razor!"

Hearing his name, Razor turned and looked at his boss, Miguel Sanchez, the mastermind behind the DEA-cartel alliance. At just thirty-one years of age, Sanchez was considered one of the most brutal drug lords the Colombian cartels had ever seen. This business with the DEA was a spinoff venture for the cartels, one that required a cold, steady hand. They had assigned the task to Sanchez, and he had proven himself worthy of their faith. Through blackmail, bribery, and butchery, he'd forged the alliance and orchestrated the pipeline. Importing narcotics had never been easier. The cartel barons were pleased by the profits rolling in at an astronomical rate under Sanchez's talented and savage fingers.

"Yeah, boss?" Razor replied, running a hand over his hairless dome. The heat and humidity of the jungle worked in harmony to soak his bare head with glistening sweat beads. He started to crave some air conditioning, but then shut that shit down. Not that he wouldn't *mind* some A/C, but *craving* it made him feel weak. And Razor was many things, but weak wasn't one of them.

"Where's the boy?" Sanchez asked.

Razor pointed at one of the outbuildings.

"Get him," Sanchez ordered. "We're moving to the estate."

"Why?"

Sanchez wore jungle khakis and carried a small riding crop that he kept slapping against the top of his polished knee-high boots. "I just received a disturbing phone call," he said. "Seems some people are giving our American friends trouble and they think those people are heading here. We will be safer at the estate."

Razor knew they were actually just as safe here at the compound, but you did not correct Miguel Sanchez unless you wanted your eyeballs blowtorched. "You really think the Americans would send someone to attack us on our own soil?" Razor scoffed at the idea. "That would be *muy estúpido.*"

"Americans are not necessarily known for their intelligence."

"Maybe it's not anybody official," Razor said. "There are mercs who specialize in rescue missions. Maybe they're just looking for the kid."

"Doesn't matter. Special Forces, mercenaries... I don't care who they are; we're moving."

"Have you talked to Jacobs?"

"Who do you think called me?"

"He's responsible for security on his end. We supplied the muscle for the hit on Reardon's wife, plus we snatched the kid ourselves. Time for Jacobs to earn his keep and do something to remedy this situation."

Sanchez nodded. "An assassin named Omega has been dispatched to track down and exterminate the problem."

"Not sure I'd call them a problem," Razor said. "More like a pain in the ass."

"They have all but destroyed our allies in the DEA," Sanchez replied. "I would call that a problem."

"And this Omega is the solution?"

"According to Jacobs, Omega is an elite operative, the best of the best. Supposedly, if Omega can't stop them, nobody can."

———

Montville, New Jersey

Despite the fact that it was early in the morning, Paul Jacobs was giving serious thought to calling his favorite escort service, the one that specialized in the rougher stuff, just the way he liked it. A face-slapping, hair-pulling, hard-bang session seemed like just the thing to take his mind off the recent string of bloody strikes that had seriously jeopardized his standing with the Colombians.

The deal had been up and running for nearly six months, nice and tidy and perfectly free of anything remotely resembling a monkey wrench. Then they snatched Reardon's kid, and it all went south. Now those involved in the operation were getting chopped and dropped by some bullet-happy sons of bitches.

Jacobs knew he had to be the next target. There was no one else left. He was the final domino, at least on this side of the Atlantic. The unlucky bastard with the big red bulls-eye. The cat in the crosshairs.

But screw these mysterious trigger-pullers, because Paul Jacobs didn't piss his pants at the first hint of danger. He didn't have a shivering, yellow-striped noodle for a spine. He was the goddamned head honcho of the DEA's Special Operations Division on the east coast, and he didn't scare easily. He'd been a warrior once, right down there in the mud and blood of the black bag trenches. A hardcore, bad to the bone hellraiser. It would take more than the boogeymen and all their bullets to make him brown his boxers.

Still, sometimes brains are better than balls, and maybe the wisest course of action would be to just give Reardon back his son. Cut their losses and call it a day. Because Jacobs was convinced that was the reason behind this sudden killing spree. It wasn't about the drugs. It was about the kid. And if they gave the kid back, Reardon would call off whatever mad dogs he had unleashed.

A moment later, he realized it was too late for that.

Auto-fire blew apart the bedroom window in his reno-vated ranch house. He didn't hear the sound of the gun, which meant a suppressor. Glass shards razored the air as slugs tattooed the walls. One of the bullets ricocheted off the solid brass lamp on the nightstand and zinged past Jacob's head.

Hot adrenalin turbocharged his bloodstream, fueling his combat instincts. He rolled off the bed. Keeping his head low, he yanked open his nightstand drawer and snatched up his Desert Eagle .44 Magnum. Way too bulky for a carry piece, but a grade-A gun for home defense, which is what he needed right now.

Apparently, Omega had been unable to track down the troublemakers. No problem. Jacobs would put .44 caliber craters where their eyes used to be and then tell Omega to go look for a job flipping burgers.

The auto-fire stopped, and now there was nothing but silence. The lack of sound worried Jacobs. What had happened to his security detail? What about the alarm system? Where the hell were the dogs? It felt like he was being attacked by fucking phantoms.

Jacobs crouched in the gray light of early morning and waited. The room's only access points were the door and the window, and he could cover them both while crouched right here in the corner. It was a solid defensive position, and he had no intention of moving.

And then a couple of fragmentation grenades whistled through the broken window like fast-pitched baseballs.

———

When Cara had sent him the names "Paul Jacobs" and "Miguel Sanchez," Kane had immediately contacted head-quarters to have Slick run down their locations. Jacobs had been easy enough to find—he lived on 19 acres in Montville, New Jersey that had once been a pumpkin farm —but Sanchez's whereabouts proved more elusive.

"DEA files indicate they have some reports that Sanchez has a compound and villa somewhere out in the jungle, but nothing substantiated," Slick said. "If you want to nail down the location, you'll need to get Jacobs to cough up the info."

"Not a problem," Kane replied. "I'm heading there now."

Thurston cut in on the conversation. "Are Reaper Two and Reaper Four with you?"

"Negative."

"You need to wait for backup, Reaper One."

"There's a kid's life at stake here," Kane said. "I'm not waiting."

"Reaper One, listen to—"

Kane cut her off. "No disrespect, but this is my call to make, not yours." Team Reaper's rules were simple enough.

Thurston controlled the missions, but when the boots were on the ground, Kane's word was law.

Thurston sighed heavily. "Fine, have it your way. Happy hunting."

Now, as he tossed the frag grenades through the broken window and then sprinted around the corner toward the front door of the house, Kane wished this was a two-man operation. They could have trapped Jacobs in a pincer move. But he stood by his decision. There hadn't been time to wait for backup. Besides, he could handle this himself. The grenades would flush his quarry, and he just needed to get inside quickly enough to intercept him.

As he moved, his eyes roved in their sockets, checking for danger. He believed he'd eliminated the guards and dogs and neutralized the alarm system, but caution came to him as naturally as breathing.

He invaded the house with his combat senses on full alert. He would not make the mistake of underestimating his opponent. Jacobs was a skilled warrior. You didn't become the head of the DEA's Special Operations Division without being the kind of man capable of taking enemy scalps.

Kane dashed through the house with his HK416 carbine leading the way, moving through the den and toward the bedroom. He heard the double bangs of the grenades popping off as he rounded a corner just in time to see Jacobs barreling down the hallway. The man was clearly expecting an ambush, for he had a Desert Eagle raised as he ran.

Kane dodged out of the line of fire as the .44 roared like a steel dragon and a bullet ripped through the space his head had occupied a heartbeat before. He immediately spun back into the hallway, knowing he would have about a one-second opening as Jacobs rode out the Desert Eagle's considerable recoil.

Sure enough, he saw the .44's muzzle elevated, Jacobs bringing it back down for another shot, his teeth bared in a savage snarl.

Kane recognized the snarl of a warrior and let out a matching snarl of his own as he hit the trigger on his HK. The controlled burst marched up Jacobs' left arm, turning the limb into a shattered mess of mangled meat.

But Jacobs proved to have some serious grit. Despite his left arm looking like something that belonged in a butcher shop wastebasket, he used his right arm to steady the Desert Eagle for a second shot.

Kane's HK spoke first. The 5.56mm NATO rounds destroyed the Desert Eagle just as Jacobs pulled the trigger. The .44 caliber round, unable to spiral through the muzzle, delivered its 750 foot-pounds of energy inside the chamber and the gun exploded. Jacobs' hand and wrist were blown to bits as thick gouts of blood splattered the floor. To his credit, Jacob didn't bellow in agony like a normal man would have; he just gritted his teeth and sucked up the pain, silently accepting that he had been bested.

Kane closed the gap between them, slinging the HK and drawing his sound-suppressed Sig. Jacobs just watched him come, helpless to do anything else. Kane pointed the gun at the man's face. "The boy," he growled. "Where is he? Don't make me ask you twice."

Jacobs' butchered arms dangled uselessly at his sides, blood streaming onto the floor. Sweat plastered his forehead, and his face had turned the color of cold ash. But he didn't look afraid; merely resigned. A man who had accepted that Death had come for him and he wasn't going to walk away alive.

Jacobs studied the pistol for a moment, then looked at Kane. "Why should I tell you?"

"You know how this works," Kane replied. "Tell me, or I'll rip the answer out of you. You're maggot food either way, but give me what I want, and I'll put you down easy. Best offer you're gonna get."

Smart enough to know when the game was up, Jacobs didn't hesitate. "Sanchez has the boy. Sent his man Razor over with a crew to do the snatch, then the crew stayed behind to take out Reardon's wife."

"You were in on all this?"

"I gave them the information they needed to pull off the grab and the hit."

Kane stared at him in disgust. "You're an officer of the law, for god's sake."

"That ship sailed a long time ago," Jacobs said. "I got greedy, and I sold out."

"Hope it was worth dying for."

"Ain't no pennies in the grave, my grandfather used to say."

"Where's Sanchez now?" Kane asked.

"Colombia."

"And the kid's with him?"

"Last I knew, they're holding him at Sanchez' compound, where they cook the coke."

"Give me the coordinates."

Jacobs rattled them off, then repeated them more slowly. Kane holstered the Sig, pulled out his phone, and quickly sent the coordinates to Swift. Then he slipped the phone back into his pocket and drew the pistol again.

They both knew the time had come.

Jacobs said, "When a man is about to die, he reflects

back on his life." He looked up at Kane. "I really fucked mine up, didn't I?"

"Yeah," Kane answered. "You sure did."

"I was a good man once," Jacobs said. "Believe it or not."

"As long as we save the kid, I'll do my best to remember you that way—a good man who just got himself twisted."

"I'd appreciate that."

There was nothing else left to say.

Jacobs sighed deeply, closed his eyes, and said, "Make it quick, will ya?"

"Sure."

The Sig bucked once, and Paul Jacobs paid the ultimate price for his sins.

A bullet knows no forgiveness.

Kane called his teammates and told them to rendezvous back at the plane. He collected any laptops, thumb drives, and cellphones he could find so that Slick could mine them for intel, then exited the house.

They'd blitzed a bloody swath of carnage up the cocaine pipeline and left the DEA portion in ruins from top to bottom, all in the name of finding Jeremy Reardon. And now that he had pinned down the kid's location, it was time to change targets.

Time to wage war against the cartels on their own turf.

Time to rain full-auto hellfire on the jungles of Colombia.

CHAPTER 8

The Sanchez estate
Colombia

Razor's bald head gleamed with perspiration as he stepped into Sanchez's office. It was hotter than the devil's cloven hooves out there, and the air conditioning offered a welcome respite from the oppressive heat. "You wanted to see me?"

Sanchez sat behind his desk, looking extremely angry. Razor steeled himself for a tongue-lashing even though he couldn't think of anything he had done to incur his boss' fury. He kept a wary eye on the leather riding crop Sanchez always carried. He had witnessed firsthand the damage the little whip could do. Wielded mercilessly—and Sanchez was nothing if not merciless—the crop could split flesh right down to the bone.

But Sanchez's first words assured Razor that he was not the target of the Colombian's rage. "The DEA end of our alliance has been smashed," Sanchez snarled. "The cartel will demand my head."

Razor didn't bother asking him to which head he was

referring, because truth was, the cartel would probably take both of them. Instead, he asked, "What do you want me to do?"

Sanchez rose from behind his desk and began pacing, tapping the riding crop against his thigh as he walked. "Nothing," he said. "Just be ready, stay alert. Whoever these *bastardos* are, they won't stop with the DEA. They will come here. They will come for the boy. They will come for us."

Razor drew his signature weapon. It practically leaped into his hand; it felt so familiar. Light gleamed along the cutthroat edge, cold and deadly, just like the man who wielded it. "They can come," he said matter-of-factly. "And they can die."

"Do not underestimate them," Sanchez cautioned. "That would be foolish, and fools have a way of dying out here."

Razor recognized the veiled threat for what it was but chose to ignore it. Wasn't like he could do anything about it anyway. Sanchez was backed by the cartels, and if he wanted Razor dead, then Razor would be dead. Such was the life he had chosen, and he would live it without regret. "I won't underestimate him," he assured his boss.

"You had better not. These *hijo de putas* are not to be taken lightly. They are a very real, very legitimate threat to us. They proved that by destroying our DEA alliance. They took no prisoners."

"We will need to rebuild," Razor said.

"First we will need to survive," Sanchez replied.

"Guess it's a good thing we changed locations," Razor remarked. "They will strike the compound first since as far as Jacobs knew, that's where the boy was being held. That will be their first target."

"So we will have advance warning that these *cabrones* are in the country," Sanchez said, "and we will be ready for them."

Razor's lips curled in a sinister smile. "But they won't be ready for us."

———

John F. Kennedy International Airport
New York

By the time Kane hustled back to JFK and hooked up with his team on the tarmac outside their HC-130, news of the latest terror attacks had gone public, along with Johnny Jihad's latest video. Footage of the George Washington Bridge destruction played in endless loops, interrupted only by shots of the Cathedral Church of Saint John the Divine, surrounded by a sea of emergency vehicles and yellow tape. Smoke wreathed the church like fog as paramedics carried the dead out under white sheets, the wheels of the stretchers rattling over shattered stone and crunching on broken glass. Every major television channel was covering the tragedy; even MTV had interrupted its regularly-scheduled reality TV programming in order to focus on the far grimmer reality out in the Big Apple.

Brick Peters was staring at his phone screen, watching one of the cable news channels, when Kane arrived. The ex-Navy SEAL shook his head at all the death and destruction. "Hell of a thing, hey, Reaper?"

"Yeah," Kane said. "It sucks dick, big time."

"I'm guessing CNN won't want to use that quote, but they should, because you make it sound positively Shakespearean."

"You think that's good, you should hear my 'Fuck yous.' Pure poetry."

Brick put away his phone. "Watching this shit makes me wish we were going after terrorists instead of cartels. I'd like to get a little payback for the good ol' U.S. of A."

"Then I've got good news," Kane said. "Thurston called just before I got here. You've been pulled off this mission and reassigned to Chief Hunt's SEAL team. Jones wants you to assist them with taking down this terrorist cell."

"Are you serious?"

"As a heart attack. They're going to run a decoy op and see if Johnny takes the bait. You'll get all the details at the briefing but looks like you're playing decoy."

Brick caught on quick. "So I'm standing in for the President."

"Looks that way."

"So if this op goes sideways, my head gets chopped off on live TV."

Kane slapped him on the shoulder. "Don't worry, I hear it only hurts for a minute."

"That's messed up, Reaper."

"You want me to get you pulled from the mission? It's not like we don't have our own job to do."

Brick shook his head. "Negative. I'll do it. Surprised they tapped me though. Thought we had a monogamous relationship with the cartels."

"You just happened to be in the right place at the right time," Kane said. "And when the President asks you to help take down the biggest terrorist in the world, you don't say no."

"You got that right."

"Good. Now get out of here. You've got a briefing to catch."

As Brick trotted off, Kane turned to Cara, Axe, and Arenas. "We need to be wheels-up in fifteen. Where's Traynor?"

The three team members exchanged glances and shuffled their feet, but nobody said anything.

Kane frowned. "Somebody want to tell me what's going on? Where's Pete?"

With a *let's get it over with* sigh, Axe said, "He's still at the hospital with Reardon."

"Are you kidding me?"

Sensing his rising anger, Cara quickly added, "Cut him some slack, Reaper. Reardon was attacked, and Pete feels he needs protection in case Omega comes back."

"We have a cartel to take down and a kid to rescue," Kane said. "The cops can handle guard duty."

"If it was your friend, would you trust his life to a couple of patrolmen?" Arenas asked. "Especially a skilled operator like this Omega seems to be? Think about it, Reaper. Put yourself in his shoes."

"We'll be facing a small army in Colombia," Kane said. "I need all the fingers on triggers I can get."

"We'll get it done," Cara assured him. "Have a little faith."

"It's not faith I want," Kane replied. "It's fucking firepower."

He turned and walked away without saying another word. The midmorning sun was starting to heat up the tarmac under his boots. When he was out of earshot of the others, he pulled out his phone and called Traynor.

The ex-DEA agent answered on the first ring. "Figured you'd be calling, boss."

"I'll make this quick," Kane said. "Reardon's your friend, so you do what you gotta do."

"Thanks. I appreciate that," Traynor said. "But the tone of your voice tells me there's a 'but' coming."

"But," Kane added, "when this mission is over, I'll be taking a hard look at whether or not I still want you on this team."

Silence on the other end, as Traynor was clearly caught off guard. When he spoke again, he said, "Kane... Reaper... c'mon, man, don't do this to me."

"I need people I can rely on," Kane said. "I get why you're sitting this one out, but the kind of people I want watching my six are the ones who don't sit out while their teammates go to war."

"Are you calling me a coward?"

"No, I'm questioning your loyalty to this team."

There was another long silence. Kane waited it out, and finally, Traynor said, "With all due respect, Reaper, I'm not sure if I want to tell you I get where you're coming from or tell you to go fuck yourself."

"Think it over," Kane replied, "and let me know when I get back. Right now, we have to go save your friend's kid."

"Sorry, Reaper. Never meant to let you down, but I've gotta do what I think is right."

"Copy that. We'll see you on the other side."

"Kick their asses, man."

"That's the plan."

Kane hung up and walked back to the others. Losing Traynor was a blow, but he couldn't force the guy to join them, and he had made the potential consequences perfectly clear. Traynor had chosen to ride the bench on this one. That decision sat wrong with Kane, so when this was over, he'd probably tell the former DEA agent to hit the road.

Axe, Cara, and Arenas looked at him expectantly as he

approached, but he shook his head to indicate he had no intention of telling them about his conversation with Traynor. He whipped his finger in a circular motion and said, "Let's roll."

The other three exchanged worried glances that Kane ignored. They followed him onto the plane, no doubt wondering if their success at smashing the DEA tentacle of the alliance was worth the price of a divided team. They had come here as brothers in arms; now they were a family torn.

Fifteen minutes later the HC-130 roared down the runway and climbed into the clear blue sky, banking toward El Paso as each person sat in silence, alone with their dark thoughts and demons.

———

Team Reaper Headquarters

They landed at Biggs Army Airfield four hours later. None of them had spoken a word on the flight. Brooke picked them up and drove them back to headquarters. Axe rode shotgun, his hand resting on her thigh the whole way. Kane rode in the back with Cara. He did not rest his hand on her thigh.

As they entered the converted warehouse that served as their headquarters, Brooke and Axe peeled off and headed for the bunks at an eager pace.

"Slow down, you two," Kane called out. "You've got a briefing in ten minutes."

Brooke tossed a smile over her shoulder, lips quirking up naughtily. "That leaves us eight minutes for a shower."

Kane grinned and shook his head. "Let's make it twenty

minutes 'til the briefing. Wouldn't want you to get cheated, Miss Reynolds." He gave her a wink.

"Thanks, Reaper." The sometimes-couple hurried off to take full advantage of their extended alone time, shedding clothes before they were even fully out of sight.

Cara watched them go. "How does Axe even have the energy?" she said to Kane. "We've been up and on-the-go for over thirty hours."

"The man's a machine."

"God bless him." Cara moved away. "I'll see you at the debriefing. I need to go find some caffeine."

Kane watched her go. No sassy, teasing sway to her backside this time. Unlike Axe, they were both just too tired to even think those kinds of thoughts. And they had miles more to go before they could rest.

He took a quick shower, put on clean clothes, and chugged a cola. None of those things exactly made him feel good as new, but they worked in tandem to make him feel at least a little refreshed, and that was good enough. Team Reaper had plenty of experience at pushing forward with minimal sleep. Weary muscles and aching bones could still carry the fight to the enemy. Once this cartel was crushed and Jeremy Reardon reunited with his father, they could all face-plant into their pillows and take twenty-four-hour naps.

He found Swift banging away on his keyboard like it owed him money while all sorts of jargon and symbols that meant nothing to Kane flashed across the quadruple monitors the computer wizard used. He turned over the electronics collected from Jacobs' residence.

"Thought you could crack those and see what sort of intel they've got on them."

Swift paused his keyboard abuse long enough to slurp

down an energy drink, then said, "I can crack 'em, no sweat. You don't need it to stand up in court, do you?"

Kane shook his head. "Nobody left alive to prosecute."

"So it was take-no-prisoners, huh?"

"That's the way it goes sometimes."

"That's the way it goes *most* of the time when you're involved," Swift said.

Kane smiled without much mirth. "They don't call us Reaper for nothing."

"Point taken."

"How you making out on that other thing?" Kane asked. "Thurston on to you yet?"

"C'mon, man," Swift scoffed. "Give me some credit. The general is super fantastic at keeping our sorry butts in line, but her computer savvy is basic at best. If I can cover my tracks from the DEA, CIA, NSA, and Pentagon, I think I can cover 'em from Thurston. I've got a data analyzation program running in the background, sifting through information on the attacks as it rolls in, and she's none the wiser."

"Jones pulled Brick for a decoy operation with some of Hunt's SEALs, so we've got some justification now to stick our noses into this, but I still prefer to keep it between you and me for now."

"No problem."

"Your program pick up anything useful?"

"Nothing yet." Swift shrugged. "Takes time. Sorry."

Kane slapped him on the shoulder. "Keep at it. Let me know if anything pops."

"You got it."

The others began filing into the briefing room, taking their seats. Axe and Reynolds entered last, looking flushed but happy. Ferrero had once approached Kane about banning inter-team romances, but Kane's stance was that as long as his people delivered in the field, he didn't care what —or who—they did in their downtime. So far neither Ferrero nor Thurston had overruled his decision.

The general buckled right down to business. "That was some nice work in New York. You guys took out the DEA component of this alliance in less than twelve hours. That, ladies and gentlemen, is impressive."

"Any fallout?" Kane asked. "This was a blitz, so we left bodies on the ground."

"And a lot of them," Thurston commented.

"We did what had to be done. Not to mention every one of those bastards deserved a bullet."

"No argument from me," Thurston assured him. "I'm working with the DEA to get everything cleaned up. As you can imagine, they've got egg on their face from all this, so they're very interested in making it all go away as quickly and quietly as possible."

"Oh, I'll bet," said Ferrero. "One thing the Agency brass was always good at was covering their asses."

"But as you know," Thurston continued, "the mission isn't over yet. We still need to rescue Jeremy Reardon and deep-six this cartel. That's why Reaper will be wheels-up in a couple hours, headed for Colombia."

"My team is down two," Kane said. "Traynor bailed, and Brick got snatched up to play with the SEALs."

Thurston nodded. "Ferrero can fill a spot."

"Do I get to shoot this time?" the ex-DEA agent inquired. "Usually you can't get a bullet in edgewise with Kane around."

"Oh, your guns will get hot on this one," Kane said. "Guaranteed."

"Then sign me up."

"I could use one more," Kane said to Thurston. "We're

hitting a manufacturing plant, and I expect it to be guarded by a small army."

"I want Reynolds here in case we need to send in a Predator," Thurston replied. "So that just leaves Teller."

Kane looked over at the big, broad-shouldered former USAF Master Sergeant. "How about it, Pete? Feel like tagging along and snorting some gunpowder?"

Teller's regular assignment on Bravo Team was UAV tech, but like all team members, he could hit the mud and blood when called upon to do so. "I was in the Air Force, remember?" he said. "I'm always up for a plane ride."

"You know there's no lobster tails, right?" Arenas asked with a grin. Teller had regaled them with tales of how fantastic the Air Force chow halls were.

Teller grinned back. "Don't worry, these days all I eat are snakes."

Axe slapped the table in approval. "A bunch of snake-eaters and ass-kickers; that's what we are."

"Damn straight," Kane said. "Now shut up and let the general finish."

Axe looked respectfully apologetic. "Sorry, ma'am."

"Don't sweat it. I appreciate the enthusiasm." Thurston motioned to Swift, who put a satellite photo of a fenced compound up on the largest monitor. "Turns out the intel Reaper got from Jacobs wasn't bullshit. There really is a manufacturing plant at the coordinates he gave us."

"So, the mission is simple," Kane said. "Go in, get the kid out, and blow the place to hell."

"The kid is priority one," Thurston agreed. "But we'd also like to take Miguel Sanchez off the board. He has a villa about ten miles from the compound."

"Jacobs said they're holding the boy at the compound,"

Kane said. "We need to hit that first. Then we can go knock on Sanchez's door and see if he's home."

"Agreed. I want that boy safe. But I also want Miguel Sanchez dead or in custody if we can pull it off."

"When it comes to scumbags like Sanchez, dead is better," Kane rasped.

"Coffin or cage, let's put him in one of them."

"How we getting in-country?" Cara asked. "The cartels will be expecting us, so you know they'll have eyes on all the major airports."

With a couple of keyboard strokes, Swift threw a photo up onto a secondary screen. It showed a square-jawed man with close-cropped, gray-streaked black hair and a matching mustache that drooped down each side of his mouth.

"Meet Paul Oswald," Thurston said. "He's a freelance pilot with ties to the merc business. He also happens to be a smuggler with his own little airstrip in the jungle, about twenty-five klicks from Sanchez's compound. The cartels either don't know about it or if they do, never bother it."

"He's probably giving them a cut," Teller said.

"You may very well be right. Or they could just not give a rip as long as he's not smuggling narcotics," Thurston said. "Either way, it's off the grid, so that's where you'll insert."

"Where'd we dig up this guy?" Arenas asked.

"The CIA put me in touch with him."

"Can we trust him?"

"The spooks use him. Take that for whatever it's worth. Plus he's a merc, and our money is good."

Axe asked, "Are we hiking the twenty-five klicks from airfield to target?"

"Negative," Thurston replied. "Once you land, you'll head to the river, about three miles, and then insert into cocaine country by boat. Oswald managed to secure us a black market SOC-R for your use. You get as close as you can with the boat, then hike the rest of the way."

"That SOC-R must have cost us a pretty penny," Ferrero said.

"It did," Thurston confirmed. "But if you're worried about saving a few bucks, I can call him back and order a rowboat instead."

"No, the SOC-R is good," Ferrero grinned.

"Thought you might say that."

SOC-R stood for Special Operations Craft-Riverine, a V-hulled, high-performance tactical watercraft designed for short-range insertion and extraction of SOF forces. It was propelled by a pair of 440HP diesel engines each driving a water pump-jet. Team Reaper had used a SOC-R on a previous mission and was familiar with its attributes.

"If we're floating down a river in bad boy country," Kane said, "I hope that SOC-R comes with a full weapons system."

"Not full," Thurston replied, "but you've got one minigun forward and one fifty-cal aft. Oswald said that was the best he could do on short notice."

"Good enough," Kane said. "That minigun is some heavy metal firepower, so we should be okay. When do we leave?"

"I've arranged clearance for Oswald to land at Biggs for pickup at sixteen-thirty hours."

Kane glanced at the clock on the wall. A 4:30 p.m. pickup gave them ninety minutes to pack up and get to the airfield. "All right, people, grab your gear and be ready to roll out in one hour." He looked pointedly at Burton and Reynolds. "And Axe, that means you don't have time to be grabbing anything else, you hear me?"

Axe grinned. "I'm good, boss."

"Yeah, that's what Reynolds keeps telling us."

With a round of good-natured laughter easing the pre-combat nerves, the team left the briefing room to prepare for war.

———

Paul Oswald's cargo plane looked like it had seen better days and those days had been somewhere circa. 1968, but the smuggler assured Kane the dents, dings, and rust were cosmetic only, gave the plane character, and that the mechanics were "tight as a dingo's arse." Kane almost asked him how he knew how tight a dingo's ass was, but then thought better of it.

Oswald's accent sounded as fake as an American trying to imitate Crocodile Dundee, but the merc assured him he was a native Aussie. "Born in Sydney, but raised in the bush, and I've got the scars to prove it," the pilot said, tapping his buttocks but offering no further explanation. "It's what makes me so bloody good at what I do."

Kane wasn't clear on how being born in the city but raised in the outback qualified someone for a life as a mercenary smuggler-pilot, but he left it alone. They were here for a ride, not chitchat. He forked over the money and said, "As long as you're good enough to get us where we need to go and get us back out without asking questions."

Oswald pocketed the cash—good old American green-backs, just like he'd insisted—and gave him a toothy smile. "Questions aren't part of the deal, mate. But I will ask you this—you know you're heading into cartel country, right?"

"Do we look like tourists to you?"

The smuggler looked at all the weapons and gear, then said, "Not exactly." He shrugged. "Your funeral, not mine."

It's going to be somebody's funeral, all right, Kane thought but kept it to himself. Oswald no doubt suspected they were going to rack up a kill-count, but there was no reason to confirm it.

Since Oswald was a one-man show, Kane rode in the copilot's seat while Cara, Axe, Ferrero, Arenas, and Teller sprawled out in the cargo hold with their gear. Kane glanced in the back and saw they were all taking power naps, resting up for the battle to come.

As the plane droned toward the setting sun, Kane looked out the window at the ocean flashing by beneath the wings and allowed himself an introspective moment.

This mission was about rescuing Jeremy Reardon. Striking a blow against the cartels was a nice bonus, but not necessary for this mission to be a success. That said, putting down Jacobs and all his corrupt cronies had been justice. And in the shadowed corners of his soul, where the spiders and demons and bad things crawled, Kane knew that gunfire justice was part of the fuel that made him tick.

He and his team were about to launch a strike into a Colombian hell-zone with saving Jeremy Reardon as the top priority. But he would be lying through his teeth if he said he didn't relish the chance to smash some coke-slingers.

No judge.

No jury.

Just bring in the executioners.

The scumbags more than deserved the hell and thunder he planned to rain down on their evil heads.

He wasn't sure what that said about him—maybe he was more bloodthirsty than he cared to admit—but he didn't need to justify his actions to anyone. Besides, they were Team Reaper, not Team Sunshine, and violent death came with the territory. They waged war against the cartels, and anyone affiliated with them, and that meant they had to kill. And it was this willingness to kill, to do what was necessary to get the job done, that made the team so effective. They hit hard, they hit fast, and nobody flinched when it was time to pull the trigger.

To save the innocent, they killed the guilty. It was as simple as that. No primrose path for Reaper and company; the road they walked was littered with the bones of the dead and the damned.

Kane gazed out the cockpit as the bright orange ball of the sun sank, and the sky began its gradual plunge into the darkness of evening. In several hours, beneath the belly of the plane would be a thick, tangled canopy comprising the harsh, unforgiving jungles of Colombia. A place where death could come in the blink of an eye, the swipe of a claw... or the pull of a trigger. Somewhere down in that green inferno was a young, innocent boy. Reaper would gun down a thousand evil men to save one innocent child, and Kane's soul would regret nothing. As a rule, drug dealers didn't deserve to keep sucking God's good air. Drug dealers who also kidnapped little kids deserved it even less. Fuck 'em all and let 'em eat bullets.

The pilot's voice snapped him back from his grim musings. "Hey, mate, you know they put a bounty on your scalp, right?"

Kane turned his head toward Oswald. Without really thinking about it, his right hand crept closer to the butt of his thigh-holstered Sig M17. He would shuck it in a heart-beat if he thought the merc pilot had betrayed them. "You looking to collect, buddy?"

The smuggler chuckled. "'Course not, ya bloody fool. I ain't no Judas. But I will admit, those cartel wankers are paying good. You must've really pissed them off."

"They might pay good," Kane said. "But their money don't spend in Hell."

Another chuckle from the Aussie. "Well, well, ain't you one tough cookie. Of course, that won't mean bugger-all if you catch a skull-splitter upside your noggin."

"Guess I'll have to make sure I duck."

"Sounds like a right proper plan you got there."

Kane decided the smuggler was just jaw-jacking to pass the time and allowed his muscles to relax. He was tired and on edge, which led him to expect the worse. Oswald was a mercenary, and mercs were all about the money, and the pilot had been paid well for his services. That didn't automatically mean the Aussie hadn't sold them out to the cartels for the bounty, but it lowered the odds. Plus Oswald seemed smart enough to realize that if he did well by them this time, they might very well use him again down the road. Lucrative repeat business trumped one-time payouts any day of the week in the merc world.

They crossed into Colombia flying low and under the cover of darkness, the night as black as squid ink. Oswald seemed unfazed, hands light on the controls, piloting the plane by instruments only. For all Kane knew, the belly of the plane was scraping the tops of the trees, and they were moments away from a crash-and-burn death. He forced himself to relax and trust the Aussie flyboy to get them safely to their destination.

To take his mind off the dangers of the nocturnal, below-radar insertion into hostile territory, Kane thought about Peters. By now the decoy operation with the SEALs would be over, one way or the other. He fired off a quick prayer to the gods of war that the big man had made it out alive. Not that he put much faith in prayer. Generally speaking, he only believed in the gun in his hand and the

men—and women—who watched his six. Still, the occasional appeal to a higher power never hurt anyone.

Mulling over things like faith and trust and who had his
back made him think of Traynor. Kane knew he had a hard
decision to make when this was over. He stared out the
window at the darkness, broken only by the reflection of the
plane's instrument panel lights.

Part of him wanted to throw Traynor on the ground,
stomp a boot heel on the back of his neck, and grind his face
in the dirt like rubbing a pissing puppy's nose in the soiled
carpet. The man had turned his back on his team in the
middle of a mission. Loyalty was their lifeblood. When the
bullets were killing, and the blood was spilling, there could
be no doubt that the person behind you had your back
without question.

That said, Kane understood that Traynor was showing
loyalty to his friend. He and Reardon had been through
some rough times together, had trudged through the blood
and guts as brothers in arms. With Reardon put down for
the count by some hardcore hitter, he needed someone to
watch his six, and Traynor had been there. It was exactly
the kind of loyalty Kane expected—*demanded*—from each
and every person on his team.

But justification aside, it didn't change the fact that
Traynor had bailed on them.

Give him the boot or give him a pass? Tough call, but
one he would have to make.

Kane turned his mind back to the mission at hand. They
would be on the ground soon, making their way toward the
compound. With luck, Jeremy Reardon would be out of
harm's way by dawn. Of course, Kane knew from personal
experience that things had a way of going sideways on these

kind of covert operations. Lady Luck could be a real fickle bitch.

By now the bastards had no doubt heard that the DEA end of the alliance had been decimated, so they would be expecting the fight to be brought to their doorstep. Just the fact that they had slapped a bounty on their heads and disseminated the information into the mercenary network pretty much confirmed Sanchez knew they were coming. But unless Oswald had sold them out, the drug lord and his minions couldn't know when they would strike.

Kane unbuckled and climbed back into the plane's cargo hold, double-checking all their equipment. The team wore black-and-green fatigues that would blend into the jungle environment. They had NVGs for navigating at night. The webbing of their ballistic combat vests held clutches of grenades, and Ka-Bar knives slung hilt-down for rapid deployment. Because if you were reaching for your blade, the fight had gone bad, and milliseconds counted.

Their Sig M17s rode low on their right thighs, and sound-suppressed HK 416 carbines with laser sights lay beside them. Extra magazines for the weapons were tucked into various pouches.

"Won't be long now," Kane said, nearly shouting to be heard over the roar of the plane's engines. "Everybody ready?"

They all gave him the thumbs up sign.

"Axe, you've got the Hawk. Think you can handle it?"

"No sweat, boss. I'm used to handling heavy equipment." He grinned wickedly.

Cara reached over and punched him in the shoulder. "Just wait until I tell Reynolds you called her heavy."

Axe's grin evaporated. "Don't you dare."

Kane fully expected Sanchez to have a small army, so they had brought along an equalizer: a Hawk MM-1 multi-round grenade launcher. The revolver-style MM-1 could be loaded with a dozen high-explosive projectiles and thanks to the semi-auto action, could fire those HE mini-bombs at 30 rounds per minute. The weapon was bulkier than Kane liked, and carting the beast through the jungle brush wouldn't be fun, but Axe was more than up to the task, and the MM-1's devastating firepower would help level the odds.

Equipment check complete, Kane returned to his copilot chair as the plane continued cruising through the night. Soon they would be in the fray once again, boots on the ground, fingers on triggers as they moved toward their target with terminal intensity. Soon they would be warrior-ghosts in the darkness of the jungle, silent and deadly until the critical moment they revealed their presence with maximum impact.

He wondered if even now, Sanchez was peering out his window, staring up at the moon and contemplating when Death would come for him, unaware that the Reaper was already on its way.

Coming to bring the pain.

Let the blood-hunt begin.

CHAPTER 9

The Atlantic Ocean

As soon as Brick saw the bodycams clipped to the terrorists' Kevlar vests, he knew Johnny Jihad was a no-show. They would have to settle for one of his sidekicks.

He was on a small fishing boat fifteen miles off Long Island, at the coordinates provided by Johnny during his televised speech. Brick had piloted the boat himself, not wanting to put anyone else in danger if the terrorists decided to just open fire when they approached. A beheading made for a more gruesome statement, but a couple of AK magazines emptied at close range got the job done quicker, and Brick wasn't sure the jihadists would be able to resist the temptation.

Following the briefing with Chief Borden Hunt, where it had been explained this was a decoy operation designed to take at least one terrorist alive, Brick had spent an hour in a chair while a movie makeup crew pulled off a rush job to make him resemble President Jack Carter. The façade wouldn't hold up under close scrutiny, but it was good enough to lure the terrorists into the trap.

Beneath the surface, clustered under the boat for concealment, were four Navy SEALs, utilizing closed-circuit breathing systems known as rebreathers to avoid bubbles that would betray their presence. Since this was not a deep-dive excursion, they were using the LAR V Draeger model, which ran on one hundred percent oxygen, filtered the carbon dioxide from the exhaled air, and were good for a maximum depth of only seventy feet.

The SEALs' waterproof earpieces allowed them to hear Brick. They would not make their move until he uttered the go-code: "Uncle Sam." When they heard those two words, they would immediately surface with their Heckler & Koch MP5N submachine guns ready for some dirty work. The HKs were currently in dry weapons bags, ready to be deployed at a moment's notice. The guns had been coated with a special lubricant to ensure they still worked despite their saltwater submersion.

Brick packed his own heat, his Sig M17 tucked into the small of his back, concealed beneath the baggy jacket he wore to hide the fact that he was bigger than President Carter, as well as to cover up the ink on his forearms. Someday there might be a tattooed POTUS, but Jack Carter was not that man.

Brick had no way of knowing, but the four terrorists—two men, two women—were the same quartet responsible for the Central Park massacre the day before. "Targets approaching now," he said, though he knew the SEALs hidden beneath him could no doubt see the hull of the terrorists' boat as it knifed its way through the water toward them.

A moment later, as the vessel drew closer, he saw the

bodycams and snarled a curse. Then he quickly passed on vital information to the SEALs. "Be advised, there's four of them, and they're wearing body armor. Headshots only. I repeat, headshots only."

The terrorists pulled up alongside him. They all had MAC-10s slung over their shoulders. None of them wore masks. No surprise there. They didn't care if he saw their faces, because they believed he was the President of the United States and fully expected him to be dead shortly, his head on a pike for the whole world to see.

Brick wore sunglasses and a baseball cap to further hide his features. So far the charade seemed to be working, even with the terrorists just a few meters away.

"So nice to see you, Mr. President," one of the men said with a smile, smug in his perceived victory. "Please join us on our boat."

Brick knew he needed to play the part. Carter was a gruff, no-nonsense man, and wouldn't meekly acquiesce to terrorist demands, even if he had actually agreed to sacrifice himself. "I like my boat better," Brick retorted. "You want me? Come over here and get me."

"You are not the one calling the shots," the terrorist replied. "You will do as you are told, or your country will suffer yet again."

"I'm here, aren't I?" He pointed at the man's bodycam. "That so your gutless coward of a leader can watch from afar instead of actually getting his hands dirty?"

"You will not speak of him in this way. He is a great man. The spirit of Osama Bin Laden has risen within him."

"Sounds like reincarnation crap to me," Brick said. It was getting hot under the wig and makeup. "Is that in the Koran?"

The terrorist ignored the jab. "He has already brought your infidel country to its knees."

Brick brayed laughter. "You stupid dumbasses. Even if you got hold of a damned nuke and wiped New York City off the planet, you wouldn't bring America to her knees. Because America kneels for no one, especially fucked-in-the-head idiots like you."

The terrorist's eyes suddenly narrowed. "You do not talk like the President of the United States."

Crap, Brick thought. Took it too far.

The terrorist leaned closer, and Brick knew the ruse was just about up. "Remove your hat."

Peters complied, tossing the ball cap into the bottom of the boat, revealing the gray-haired wig he wore. He reached up and ruffled the fake hair. "Satisfied?"

"Your sunglasses... take them off."

"Oh, for the love of..." Brick stretched out his hand. "Just help me onto your stupid boat and let's get this over with. If I'm going to Hell, I want to at least get there in time for supper."

The terrorist eyed him suspiciously for another few heartbeats, then shrugged and reached out his hand to help Brick-cum-President Carter step from his boat to theirs.

As Brick grabbed the terrorist's hand, he suddenly yanked the bastard off balance and rasped, "Uncle Sam sends his regards."

With his left hand, he reached behind him and drew the Sig.

His job was to keep one of the terrorists alive. The SEALs were the lethal option.

Caught off guard, the other three jihadists scrambled to bring their guns into play. Brick fired a round into his terrorist's leg, shattering the femur, crippling him instantly. As he dragged the bleeding, screaming terrorist into his boat, the SEALs surfaced. Water streamed from the lubricated muzzles of their HKs as they spat point-blank death. The remaining three terrorists went down with weeping holes drilled in their skulls as 9mm NATO rounds cored through bone and brains.

Brick silenced the howling, leg-shot terrorist by pistol-whipping him across the back of the skull, knocking him out. He quickly zip-tied his wrists and ankles. Part of him just wanted to toss the guy overboard and call it a day, but he knew he couldn't do that. He yanked the bodycam off the vest, held it up to his face, and delivered a message to Johnny Jihad who he had no doubt was on the other end watching the live feed.

"We're coming for you, asshole."

Then he crushed the camera beneath his boot heel.

The SEALs slipped back down below the surface where a mini-sub waited to take them back to shore. Brick shrugged off the jacket and stripped off the wig. His shirt was soaked with sweat, both from sun and tension. He pointed the boat toward land and shoved the throttle forward as the sun slipped lower on the horizon. Soon the sea would be dark, just like the rage coiled inside him. Johnny Jihad hadn't taken the bait, and now more people were going to die.

Brick punched the console in frustration, bruising his knuckles, as the boat raced across the waves.

———

Sitting safe and comfortable in his sanctuary, Johnny Jihad watched the feed from the bodycams as the fake President Carter and some operators—SEALs, he assumed—took down his four jihadists. They left one alive, which could only mean one thing—they intended to interrogate him in the hopes of finding out Johnny's location.

He chuckled at such foolishness. His followers had no idea where he holed up. The U.S. government could—and no doubt would—torture the man and inject him with whatever chemical concoction they used for truth serum these days, but the man could not tell them what he did not know.

He picked up a cell phone and sent a three-word text:

ONE POLICE PLAZA

Once he received notification that the message had been received, he destroyed the phone. Burners were cheap, and he had no intention of being taken down by something as stupid as a cell phone trace.

The text ensured that by tomorrow morning, the New Babylon would once again be engulfed in fire and fury. They would pay for today's deception. They would reap the brutal reward for their treachery.

President Carter liked to play tricks. Before long, Johnny would make the bastard's head disappear from his shoulders. The leader of the godless infidels would die screaming, and the world would watch. Then they would know that Al-Qaeda was not to be trifled with.

Johnny sat back and smiled to himself. Tomorrow New York City would suffer another Armageddon.

———

The White House

President Jack Carter stood behind his desk in the Oval Office and gazed out the three large windows that faced the south lawn, silently praying for the mental fortitude to guide the country through the nightmare now gripping it. He wasn't prone to pity parties, but this had to be the worst crisis any modern day president had ever faced. Five terrorist attacks in two days—with another one threatened for tomorrow—had left the nation shaken to its very core. He reached deep down inside, way down where a man found out what he was really made of and grabbed hold of strength and serenity.

Then Hank Jones walked in, and the serenity went straight to hell.

"Just heard from Chief Hunt," Jones said without preamble. "Three terrorists dead, one captured. None of them are Johnny."

The President felt his heart sink, and his guts churn. He turned away from the window with a deep sigh. "Are we sure?"

"Given that the bastard wears a mask, it's impossible to be one hundred percent sure, but two of the terrorists were women, so we can rule them out. The one we captured made comments inferring Johnny wasn't with them. Plus, the terrorists that showed up at the decoy site wore body-cams, which indicates someone—presumably Johnny—was watching from afar. All of this makes us pretty confident Johnny is still at large."

"Guess it was too much to hope that he would actually take the bait," Carter said. "We couldn't get that lucky."

"It was always a long shot. We knew that going in," Jones replied. "But we took one alive, so maybe we can get some information out of him that'll lead to Johnny."

"Where is he now?"

Jones stared at him stone-faced. "With all due respect, Mr. President, do you really want me to answer that question?"

Carter thought about it for a moment, then waved a hand. "Forget I asked. Plausible deniability might come in handy when this is all over." But then he gave Jones a hard-eyed look. "But Hank?"

Jones stood ramrod straight, knowing what was coming. "Yes, sir?"

"Whatever it takes. Understand?"

Jones nodded. "Affirmative, Mr. President. Whatever it takes."

"Good." Carter inwardly began the process of learning to live with what he had just ordered. "Because unless we can break this man quickly, many more people are going to die tomorrow morning."

"One broken terrorist, coming right up," Jones promised grimly.

CHAPTER 10

Colombia

Team Reaper wasted no time exiting the plane once it touched down in Colombia and rolled to a stop near a corrugated metal hangar so covered with thick, snake-like vines that it looked like it had been carved directly out of the jungle. It might have been night, but the air was still hot and humid.

As they geared up, Oswald pointed to a barely-discernable footpath next to the hangar. "Follow that trail there, and it'll take ya right to the boat."

Kane asked, "You sure it'll be there?"

The smuggler arched his eyebrows. "You want me to swear on my mum's dear, departed soul or something, mate?"

"Swear on whatever you want," Kane said. "But I need to know that boat's gonna be there."

"It'll be there. I put it there myself."

"If it's not..."

"Yeah, yeah." Oswald waved dismissively. "You'll hunt

me down and do horrible things to me." He grinned crookedly. "Not my first rodeo, cowboy."

"Good," Kane replied. "Then you won't mind me doing this." His left hand shot out, grabbed the mercenary by the back of the neck, and pulled him close. At the same time, his right hand drew his Sig and rammed the muzzle under the man's chin.

Oswald was smart enough to hold very still. "Seriously, mate... what the hell?"

"I'm gonna need you to tell me how many cartel soldiers are waiting for us at that boat."

"Are you kidding me right now, ya bleedin' bastard? Are you seriously accusing me of selling you out?"

"Damn right I am." Kane pressed even harder on the pistol. "How many?"

"None, ya crazy dingo! How many times I gotta tell ya? I didn't sell you out!"

"I don't believe you."

"Not my bloody problem!"

"It's gonna be your problem when I pull this trigger and pop a hole in your skull."

Oswald suddenly deflated, muscles loose, arms dangling limply by his side. All the fight just went right out of him. If not for the gun tucked under his chin propping him up, he might very well have sunk to the ground. "Okay," he said, his tone sorrowful and full of regret. "You got me, mate. Don't go jacking up my head with a bullet. I'll tell you the truth."

"I'm listening," Kane said.

The Aussie merc took a deep breath, then bellowed at the top of his lungs, "I didn't sell you out! That's the damn truth! Stick it up your arse and eat it, ya bleedin' gob!" He locked eyes with Kane, glaring defiantly as if daring him to pull the trigger.

Kane wasn't one to back down from a hostile staring contest. He glared right back, letting the smuggler see the cold menace glittering in his eyes like ice chips. Then he abruptly grinned and lowered the Sig. "Well, why didn't you say so?" He patted the pilot on the shoulder and stepped back.

Oswald gaped at him like a fish that can't believe it just escaped the hook. "Really? You were just screwing with me?"

"Not screwing with you. Making sure you were telling the truth."

"I oughta sock you right in the jaw, mate."

"You can try," Kane said. "But it won't end well for you. Of course, you already know that, since this ain't your first rodeo."

Oswald shook his head and chuckled. "Bugger my hole, but I like your style."

Kane offered his hand. Not the one holding a gun. "No hard feelings?"

The merc shook his hand. "The only thing hard is my willy. Forgot to tell ya, I kind of like it when men get rough with me." He gave Kane a wink.

Kane laughed and holstered the Sig. "Thanks for understanding."

"Hey, what're ya gonna do, right? It's not like you slapped me across the forehead with your pecker."

"Thought about it." Kane grinned. "But I didn't want to cave in your skull."

Oswald snickered. "You're a funny bloke and that ain't no lie." He motioned toward the trail. "Go on, get outta here. I'll be here waiting for whoever makes it back."

"You don't think we're all coming back?"

The merc snorted. "Mate, there's six of you going up against a cartel army. I'll be shocked if even one of you makes it back alive. And even if one does, I'll be expecting them to come back missing at least two limbs." He shook his head. "You guys are on a suicide mission."

"What can I say?" Kane replied. "Guess we just don't fear the Reaper."

———

The White House

Nick Pullman, the White House Chief of Staff, muted the television in the Oval Office and turned to President Carter. "It's not good, sir."

"Just give it to me straight, Nick."

Pullman took a deep breath and then plunged ahead. "The latest polls show that the American public thinks you botched this one up."

"What the hell do they want me to do? Turn myself over to the terrorists?"

"Actually..." Pullman replied. "...yes."

"Let me guess—it was a CNN poll."

"CNN, Fox News, Washington Post, Gallup... it's unanimous, Mr. President. Averaging all the polls together, nearly 58% of Americans think you should sacrifice yourself to stop the attacks."

Carter leaned back in his chair. "Huh," he grunted. "Well, isn't that just swell."

The bodycam footage showing the decoy operation —complete with remarkably clear shots of Brick Peters as the fake President—had been leaked to the news media shortly after 8:00 p.m. and had been playing on a seemingly endless loop ever since. Accompanying the footage was another video from Johnny Jihad, still wearing his hooded mask in front of the shredded American flag. His message was short and anything but sweet.

"As you can see, your cowardly President, instead of surrendering himself to me and ending the death and destruction I have rained down upon your heads, has chosen trickery and deception. Tomorrow America will once again run red with infidel blood. You were warned. Now you will pay."

President Carter turned his head and looked at the muted television. On the screen, Brick was in the act of shooting the terrorist in the leg. He gestured at the TV. "Don't the American people understand the mission was at least a partial success? We captured one of the bastards. He's being interrogated as we speak."

"None of that will matter if there's another attack tomorrow," Pullman replied. "Unless the prisoner gives us information that stops the attacks, the public is going to view today's operation as a debacle."

"And I'm sure my opponents are falling all over themselves to point fingers and shovel all the blame onto me," Carter said sourly.

Pullman nodded. "It's already starting, sir. In fact, some of your detractors are already starting to whisper the I-word."

"Impeachment? Are you kidding me?" Carter snapped. "I authorized a covert mission to try to apprehend the most wanted terrorist on the planet. We not only killed three members of his cell, but we also managed to take one alive for questioning. How is that impeachable?"

"I didn't say it was," Pullman replied. "I said some of your political opponents are throwing it around."

"The hell with 'em."

"I know caution is not your strong point, sir, but I'd tread lightly with that kind of mentality," the Chief of Staff advised. "The country has been hit by five catastrophic attacks in two days. Speaking bluntly, the majority of Americans don't like you right now. If your opponents can rally enough support from the people on pursuing impeachment, you might find your neck on the political chopping block." He paused, then added, "Frankly, sir, if we're hit by another attack tomorrow, the demands for your resignation are going to be very loud."

"Then let's stop another attack from happening," Carter said. "What's the status on the interrogation of the prisoner? Has he given us anything useful yet?"

Pullman pressed the intercom and said, "Send in General Jones, please."

Hank Jones entered the Oval Office a few moments later. He looked sick and angry.

President Carter frowned. "Hank, are you all right?"

"No, sir. I'm actually a pretty long way from all right."

"What's wrong?"

"We lost him."

"Lost who?"

"The prisoner. The terrorist."

Carter's frown deepened. "What do you mean, lost him? Where is he?"

"He's dead."

"Damn it!" Carter exploded. "I told you to get answers, not kill him."

"We didn't kill him," Jones said. "He killed himself.

Suicide pill. A false tooth with a cyanide capsule underneath."

"A cyanide capsule? That's an old-school play right there."

"Simple but effective."

The President rubbed his face dejectedly. "So we lost our one shot at stopping this next attack. Now, what do I do? Jump on Twitter and ask for hopes and prayers?"

"God and luck, sir," Jones replied. "That's about all you've got right now."

"So I need a miracle," President Carter sighed. "Looks like we're royally screwed."

———

Colombia

Kane's time as a recon marine had instilled in him a combat-centric sixth sense that alerted him to danger. His days with Team Reaper working under the World Wide Drug Initiative had honed that sixth sense to a razor-sharp edge. He had learned long ago to never ignore it. And right now, that sixth sense was banging alarm bells in his brain, letting him know that someone or something in the vicinity meant them harm.

He estimated they were less than a quarter-klick from where the SOC-R was supposed to be. The wet, pungent smell of the river permeated the jungle here. It was a smell he knew all too well—and one he hated—from his previous missions here. He'd always hated Colombia, and that would never change. One of his least favorite places on earth.

Through his NVGs, Kane could see that the path, not much wider than a game trail, curved around a bend up ahead. The jungle pressed thick on both sides, reducing visibility to just a few meters. Kane raised a clenched fist, signaling everyone to hold fast. He motioned Axe forward as Cara dropped and pivoted to watch their back trail, HK416 carbine tucked tight to her shoulder. Arenas crouched beside her, rifle sweeping a ninety-degree vector. Ferrero and Teller each took one side of the trail, eyes looking through their NVGs to probe the dense, tangled brush just beyond the ends of their muzzles.

Kane kept his HK pointed forward as Axe edged up next to him and asked, "What's up, Reaper?"

"Got a bad feeling that we're not alone." Kane kept his voice low.

"If it makes you happy, I don't think you're wrong."

"In this case, I'd rather be wrong."

"Think there's an ambush around the bend?"

"Good place for it."

Axe nodded. "If I was planning an ambush, that's where I'd do it."

Kane made the call. "Off trail the rest of the way."

"Copy that."

As Axe moved back to pass the word to the others, auto-fire came slashing out of the jungle. The salvo caught Arenas on the left side, two bullets ripping into his upper thigh. Another one snuck in just below his vest, struck a rib, and deflected rearward to tear a nasty chunk out of his side. He grunted in pain as the impacts drove him sideways into Cara.

She returned fire, blazing blindly into the brush as she shouted, "Reaper Three is down!"

"Son of a bitch!" Kane snarled. "Cara, Teller, cover

Arenas! Everyone else, get off the trail and find these motherfu—"

Another burst of auto-fire, this one from a different position, shut him up by thumping a trio of slugs into his vest. The blows kicked him off his feet and he hit the ground with the breath knocked out of him. His chest felt like he'd been hit by a wrecking ball. Pain surged through him, but he knew he was a sitting duck out here on the open trail.

Get up! he silently screamed at himself. Fighting through the hurt, he dragged himself into the brush.

Through the green tint of his NVGs, he saw Axe and Ferrero diving into the jungle. Cara and Teller fired controlled bursts into the jungle, letting their HKs tell the unseen attackers exactly what they thought of their bushwhack tactics.

Kane stayed prone, hidden under a cluster of ferns, struggling to regain his breath. This wasn't the first time he'd caught a round in the Kevlar and probably wouldn't be the last, but it pissed him off every time. Not to mention he would have a bowling-ball-sized bruise on his sternum for the next couple of weeks.

Off to his right, he heard the *phut-phut-phut* of suppressed gunfire. Someone cried out in pain, followed immediately by another short burst, then Axe's voice came through the com. "Tango down."

More auto-fire on the other side of the trail. Cara's gun added to the violent cacophony, accompanied by Teller. They were burning through their second magazines, fighting furiously to keep the attackers away from the wounded Arenas.

Kane summoned enough breath to call out, "Anybody got eyes on the tangos?"

Zeroing in on the sound of his voice, bullets scythed into the ferns and drilled divots in the dirt beside him.

"Shit!" Kane rolled away from the tracking line of fire. He used the momentum to power up into a combat crouch, spinning toward the threat as his HK sought target acquisition.

The guy was less than three meters away, dressed in ratty camo, glowing like a green ghost through the NVGs. The IMI Galil submachine gun in his hands swung toward Kane as he tried to hurriedly correct his aim.

Kane beat him to the punch, quicker on the trigger. His rising close-quarters burst caught the gunner low, chopping open his belly before marching up his body to explode his face into a hammered mess. The man staggered backwards, dead on his feet.

"Tango two down!" Kane said into the com. "How many more?"

From the other side of the trail, Ferrero's carbine cooked off a suppressed burst and ripped a scream from his target. "Tango three down!"

"Can't see shit in here, Reaper!" Axe said.

A sub-gun rattled to life.

"Damn it!" Cara cursed. "We're still taking fire! That last burst just missed me!"

"Copy, Reaper Two," Kane replied. "Reaper Four, Bravo Three, converge on her position. Keep your eyes peeled for bogeys. I'll circle around."

"Copy that, Reaper One."

Kane rose from his crouch, head on a swivel, and quickly scanned his surroundings. Satisfied there were no other attackers in his immediate vicinity, he crossed to the other side of the path. As he did, he glimpsed Cara, Teller, Axe, and Ferrero shielding their wounded comrade, HKs bucking as they laid down cover fire, probing the dense brush with streams of 5.56mm bullets. Then he was back in the jungle, ghosting toward the unseen gunner.

Another sustained fusillade rang out.

"He missed again," Axe said over the com. "Be advised, Reaper One, I don't think the guy has got a line of sight on us. He's just firing blind and hoping for the best."

"Copy that, Reaper Four." Kane adjusted his movements to take himself further into the jungle. The hidden gunner had to be close enough to the trail for his bullets to penetrate all the brush, but far enough back to remain concealed.

"Going prone," Kane said, dropping onto his stomach. "Shoot high and keep the bastard's head down."

His teammates immediately complied, filling the jungle with lead as Kane snaked forward, looking for a sign, any sign, of the target. Up ahead, he could see leaves and limbs exploding as bullets pulverized them.

A second later, the enemy gunner returned fire.

Kane saw the muzzle flash light up the night less than fifteen meters in front of him.

Gotcha.

Still prone, he lifted his carbine and cut loose with some full auto rock 'n' roll, emptying his magazine just behind the spot where he had seen the muzzle flash. Through the thick brush, he glimpsed fragments of thrashing movement as the bullets pounded into the target.

"Tango four down," he said into the com, standing up and heading toward the gunner's last known position. "Moving in. Hold your fire."

"Copy that, Reaper One," Axe confirmed. "Holding fire."

Kane walked over and found the guy lying in a pool of

blood, dead beyond any doubt. Kane had sent over twenty rounds downrange, and it looked like at least half of them had struck home, shearing through the ribcage and ripping away half his skull.

Some might have called it overkill.

Kane called it getting the job done.

And payback for Arenas, damn straight.

He rejoined the others on the trail. While he had been checking on the corpse, they had been checking on Arenas' injuries. "What's the sit-rep?" he asked.

"One busted rib, one broken leg, and plenty of tissue and muscle damage," Cara reported. "Bullets missed the femoral and didn't penetrate any vitals, but he's still a mess."

"I'm fine," Arenas growled, but he was unable to hide the pain in his voice.

Cara looked at Kane. "He's not going anywhere, Reaper."

"Just get me a goddamned branch to use as a crutch," Arenas said. "I can make it."

Kane crouched down in front of him and put a hand on his shoulder. "That's some impressive macho bullshit, but you and I both know the party's over for you. Sorry, man, but that's the way it is."

"C'mon, Reaper..."

Kane cut him off. "Not up for discussion. You're down for the count on this one."

Arenas slammed his fist on the ground in frustration, then sighed. "Fine, you're the boss."

"Let Cara patch you up, then we'll get you off the trail and as comfortable as possible."

Teller frowned. "We're not leaving him alone, are we?"

Kane stood up and shook his head. "No."

"I don't need a babysitter," Arenas complained, then winced as Cara started tending to his wounds. "Besides, you need all the guns you can get."

"He's not wrong," Ferrero commented.

"I know he's not wrong," Kane said. "But that doesn't change the fact that I'm not leaving a wounded man alone with hostiles in the area."

"Think they were cartel hitters?" Axe asked. "Did Oswald sell us out?"

Ferrero replied, "The one I put down had on ratty clothes and beat up boots, nothing like cartel soldiers would wear. My guess, these guys were just bandits, probably ex-guerilla fighters. Probably saw the SOC-R up ahead at the river and figured a boat like that, somebody would come for it soon, and set up an ambush to take us out."

"They did a lousy job of it," Teller said.

"Not really," Kane countered. "They took out Arenas and managed to put a couple in my chest."

Axe reached over and punched him in the vest. "Let's hear it for Kevlar, huh?"

Kane managed to hide how much the punch hurt. "Yeah," he said. "God's gift to snake-eaters."

Once Cara had splinted Arenas' broken leg, wrapped his busted rib, and used skin glue from their first aid kits to close the wounds as best she could, they carried him into the jungle far enough that he couldn't be seen from the trail. Cara suggested it would be best if he was lying down, but he flat-out refused, so they propped him against the bole of a large ceiba tree. They set his carbine on one side of him and his pistol on the other.

Kane said, "Teller, I'm gonna have you stay behind with him."

"You sure about that, Reaper? Leaves only four of you going up against a cartel army."

"There's a kid out there, probably scared to death right now. I'm not turning back." Kane looked each of them in the eye, one at a time. "But anyone who thinks this is a suicide run, you're free to bow out. No shame, no hard feelings."

Axe muttered, "No balls would be more like it."

"I don't have any balls," Cara said.

Axe gave her a look of respect. "Sister, you got the biggest balls of us all." He turned to Kane. "Shut up with all the noble you-don't-have-to-do-this crap and let's get our butts in gear. We need to hit that compound before dawn, and we've still got miles to go."

Kane didn't waste any more time talking about it. They had made their decision. They were warriors, and they would do what warriors do—refuse to back down. "Then let's hit the road," he said. "We've got a boat to catch."

CHAPTER 11

The Sanchez estate

Miguel Sanchez looked at his chirping cell phone on a nearby table with irritation. He viewed the phone as a necessary nuisance at the best of times, but right now it was about as welcome as a pit viper in your pantry. He had abducted a young girl from the nearby village and was forcing her to give him a private striptease. The girl's back and thighs bore the bleeding welts from his riding crop, a crisscrossed patchwork of hurt and humiliation. She had been stubborn, this one, and required an extra dose of persuasion before starting her performance. Her dancing lacked sexiness but the tears streaming down her face more than compensated. Her pain turned him on even more than her firm breasts and gyrating hips.

But now the show had to be stalled because some fool had picked a most inopportune time to contact him. As he picked up the phone, he vowed that if the call was not important, he would have the caller's manhood hacked off with a rusty butter knife.

He held the phone to his ear and growled, "Who is this and what do you want?"

The voice that replied was cold and flat. "Jacobs told me to contact you if things went sideways. Given all the dead bodies lying around, including Jacobs, I think it's safe to say that sideways is exactly where things have gone."

"Who are you?" Sanchez demanded.

"You can call me Omega. I'm the asset that Jacobs dispatched to handle Team Reaper."

"Who's Team Reaper?"

"I'll skip the technical details and just call them a bunch of badasses."

"Vigilantes or mercs?"

"Neither. Covert task force."

"Then how do you know about them?"

"Let's just say I have my ways," Omega replied.

"Who put them on to us?"

"The name Reardon ring a bell?"

"Of course," Sanchez replied. "We're holding his *hijo* until he gives us a list of narcs."

"Guess he went with option B."

"Then his son is dead. Reardon was warned. Now he will see that I am a man of my word."

"Hold off on that. We need the boy for bait."

"For who?"

"For Reaper, Mr. Sanchez. Who else?" The sneer in Omega's voice made it clear he thought Sanchez was a moron.

The drug baron did not suffer insolence well. "You watch your tone of voice with me, Omega."

"Spare me your threats. You've got more important things to worry about than my tone of voice. We believe Reaper made it into Colombia. So don't kill the kid. Let them come to you. Sucker them into a trap and then exterminate them. Or, if you find yourself backed into a corner, use the kid as a bargaining chip."

"They're here? In Colombia?"

"That's what I just said."

"Then I will kill them," Sanchez said with all the savagery he could muster. "I will succeed where you failed, and then you will wipe that sneer from your voice, for I will have proven myself to be the better man. I have no fear of these Reapers."

"Then you're an idiot."

"Hey, nobody talks to me that w—"

Omega hung up on him.

Sanchez stared at the phone in disbelief and silently vowed to make the man pay for his disrespect. First, he would take down these Reaper *bastardos* and then this Omega would join them in Hell. No one spoke to Miguel Sanchez with such insolence and lived to tell about it. He would make sure Omega choked to death on his own spleen.

But first, this Team Reaper needed to be put down like mad dogs.

———

Colombia

In that eerie hour between night and dawn, when dark still dominates but light has begun to bleed into the sky, four armed-to-the-teeth warriors moved in near silence along the edge of the clearing that contained Sanchez's processing plant and warehouse. Kane, Cara, Ferrero, and Axe had beached the SOC-R five klicks downriver and hiked the rest of the way. They were soaked in sweat from their trek through the jungle—especially Axe, who had to lug the Hawk MM-1—but they shrugged off the discomfort.

It was time to hunt.

Kane knew, both from training and personal experience, that predawn was the perfect killing time. Night sentries were fatigued, which sapped their alertness. At shift's end, they would be thinking about sleep, their attention subpar. Numbness crept over them, dulling that critical edge, leaving them ripe for the slaughter.

Kane crouched in the underbrush and waited, black-bladed Ka-Bar combat knife gripped firmly in his fist, ready to strike.

He didn't have to wait long.

Within minutes, a sentry strolled by, fatigue visible on his drooping face. His shoulders slumped, an AK-47 dangling haphazardly from a leather sling. His feet dragged as he shuffled tiredly toward the front gate, no doubt ready for his tour of duty to end.

Kane intended to end more than that.

He let the sentry walk past before attacking. Then he powered to his feet, snaked an arm around the man's neck, and crushed his throat to cut off any cry of alarm. The knife came up hard and fast. Using all his strength, Kane drove the sharp, heavy blade into the base of the man's skull, punching deep. Then he dragged the body into the under-brush and wiped the knife clean on the dead man's shirt.

One down, Kane thought. Who knows how many more to go.

Kill completed, the team crept toward the main gate, manned by two cartel soldiers with assault rifles. To the right of the gate loomed a twenty-five-foot guard tower with a .50 caliber machinegun mounted on top, manned by another sentry.

Kane motioned to Cara.

The former deputy from Retribution, Arizona nodded and double-checked the suppressor on the HK416. Not the most ideal sniping weapon but it would suffice. Her job was to take out the machine-gunner, which would be the signal for Axe and Ferrero to smoke the two sentries. The kills needed to be synchronized. The distance was approximately 60 meters, well within the rifle's effective range and Cara's shooting abilities.

Concealed by a patch of ferns, black-and-green fatigues blending into the shadows, Cara braced the HK across her left forearm. Through her NVGs, she saw the laser sight settle on her target. She smoothly stroked the trigger and sent a bullet sizzling up into the machinegun nest. The suppressor reduced the shot to little more than a *phytt!* sound.

Kane saw the machine-gunner's head snap back as the 5.56 NATO round burrowed in under the man's jaw and ripped up into his brain. He crumpled out of sight as red mist spritzed the air.

Less than two seconds later, Axe and Ferrero put down the pair of guards. The first one never knew what hit him as he caught a bullet in the face. Sucking oxygen one second, sucking sulfur the next.

His partner died a half-heartbeat later. A suppressed round split open the bridge of his nose and blasted through his sinus cavity before smashing out the back of his skull. Both sentries hit the ground, dead.

Kane scanned the area to confirm there were no more immediate threats, then motioned them forward.

The team rose in unison and moved stealthily toward

the gate, weapons at the ready for any surprises. A burst of hushed bullets made short work of the lock and let them inside the kill-zone, death dealers on a mission of unfettered violence.

Axe swapped his HK416 for the Hawk MM-1, all twelve cylinders stuffed with grenades. No tear gas or flash-bangs; they weren't here to show mercy, so every chamber contained a high-explosive mini-bomb, ready to unleash hell at thirty rounds per minute.

Ready to give Sanchez's goons a taste of the flames.

A luckless soldier chose that moment to emerge from an outhouse about fifty meters away, belt unbuckled, zipping up his fly. It would be the last dump the man would ever take. Kane's 5.56mm salvo blew apart the soldier's chest. The hammering impacts drove the victim back into the outhouse and dumped his dead body back onto the crapper.

The team moved across the compound like shadowed wraiths. The processing lab was on the far side, but first, they needed to take out the barracks, looming on their left. Better to kill the bad guys in their bunks than face them out in the open. Granted, there was no honor in that, but they didn't care about honor, they cared about survival. Neutralize the threat as quickly as possible.

Axe fired on the run, putting three grenades through the windows. "Fire in the hole!" he growled. Moments later, glass shattered, and doomed men screamed. The three deto-nations thundered one right after the other, blowing out all the remaining windows. Splintered debris vomited from the openings along with blown-off limbs propelled on tongues of flame and smoke. Pieces of wet meat and charred bone rained down.

The barracks door flew open, and survivors began

pouring out, some armed, some not. They stumbled about like dazed zombies, shocked and confused.

Axe lobbed two more grenades in their midst, and their disorientation turned to terror.

The HE rounds exploded, and body parts flew everywhere. Blood sprayed and spurted from savaged flesh. Two soldiers not killed outright in the blast writhed in agony on the ground until Kane and Cara snapped bullets into their heads to put them out of their misery.

Almost immediately another group of soldiers staggered out of the barracks. The lead man emerged just in time to catch a 40mm projectile square in the chest. The grenade punched through his sternum and detonated inside his chest cavity. The man evaporated in a chunky crimson mess, blown apart from the inside out.

Kane, Cara, and Ferrero poured on withering streams of auto-fire to keep the soldiers pinned inside as Axe dumped his last five rounds through the doorway. The grenades wreaked high-explosive havoc inside the barracks that caused the walls to visibly buckle. Flames lapped hungrily at the dry wood, and the conflagration spread rapidly. Anyone who tried to come out the door got cut down, and within moments, the stacked bodies blocked egress. The troops trapped inside screamed in agony as they burned alive.

"Let's move," Kane said. With the bulk of the enemy troops decimated, they needed to take down the cocaine cookhouse and find Jeremy Reardon.

Axe tossed the empty Hawk MM-1 and switched back to his HK416.

They skirted the burning barracks and approached the lab at a fast trot. Kane opted for a full-frontal assault, kicking open the door and charging in low with his assault rifle blazing. Axe, Cara, and Ferrero followed hot on his heels.

Only one guard defended the four white-clad chemists. The guy managed to squeeze off a hasty burst with his sub-gun, but it missed by a good margin, ripping into the wall to Kane's right.

Kane's aim proved much more accurate and far more lethal. He tracked a line of auto-fire across the soldier's torso. The sizzling salvo slammed the target across a work-bench. His crashing corpse knocked over several containers of chemicals which mingled with his fresh-spilled blood.

All four chemists raised their hands to show they were unarmed, but Reaper was taking no prisoners. The hell with these coke cookers. They dealt in white poison, their work bringing misery and death to thousands of people. They profited from those deaths, and now it was time for them to reap the consequences.

"Light 'em up," he rasped.

The Reaper warriors chopped them down with their HKs.

As the bodies hit the floor, Team Reaper ejected their spent magazines and slapped in fresh ones. Kane plucked a couple of incendiary grenades from his combat webbing and tossed them onto a workbench. As the team headed for the door, the grenades went off behind them and sent thermite in all directions. The burn-baby-burn conflagration would leave nothing but charred wreckage and hot ashes in its wake.

As they started to exit, gunfire greeted them, and bullets chewed the air, courtesy of a trio of soldiers who had popped up from out of nowhere. Kane retreated inside the cookhouse, pushing the others back with him. "Three tangos outside," he informed them.

Chemical-laced smoke was quickly filling the cocaine lab. Coughing as the fumes burned her throat, Cara said, "We can't hole up here, Reaper."

"I know." Kane could feel the rapidly-spreading flames at their backs. They couldn't stay in here much longer unless they liked their ribs barbecued.

He spun back into the doorway, catching the soldiers off guard, and terminated the nearest target with a precision burst from his HK that tore off the top of the guy's head.

The other two soldiers directed twin streams of lead toward Kane's position. He ducked back inside for cover as slugs drilled into the doorway, gouged splinters from the jamb, and pocked the wall around it. The flames were uncomfortably close as he waited out the thunder of guns.

And then the gunfire stopped, followed by the distinct sound of magazines being ejected. Kane's lips peeled back from his teeth in a cold, knowing grin. The two fools should have alternated firing. Instead, fueled by fear, they had emptied their clips at the same time. Now they were both frantically trying to reload.

Reaper seized the moment and made them pay for their tactical error.

Kane charged out the door and hammered a sustained burst of 5.56mm heart-stoppers into the torso of the man on the left. Close on his heels, Cara took out the guy on the right with a short, chopping burst to the chest. Both soldiers toppled backwards into the dirt, blood clouding the air above their twitching corpses.

"Well, that sucks," Axe said, nudging Ferrero. "We didn't even get to play."

"Don't worry," Kane said grimly. "You'll get your chance."

Flames totally engulfed the barracks, thick black smoke

rolling across the compound, and the lab was quickly becoming an inferno. The team moved toward the warehouse, cold-eyed warriors wreathed in smoke like death-demons strolling through the scorched landscape of Hell.

Jacobs had told Kane that Jeremy Reardon was being held in a storage shed. Various small buildings—storage units, basically—littered the compound. The team searched each one as they circled toward the warehouse in the northwest corner. The search confirmed what Kane's gut already knew—Jeremy wasn't here. Inside one of the sheds, they found a grimy mattress and some food remnants, and it didn't take a genius to figure out that at one point this had been the kid's cage. But since he wasn't there, he had either been moved elsewhere or killed, and as soon as they finished burning this place to the ground, Kane intended to find out which.

There were four sentries guarding the warehouse, but Reaper's team cut them down with ruthless efficiency before Axe prepped the cocaine-filled building for destruction. The C-4 charges would be more than enough to level the warehouse and leave nothing but a burning hell-zone behind. Axe set the timers for two minutes, and the team exfiltrated the smashed compound.

They were well into the jungle when the C-4 detonated. They couldn't see the actual explosion, but a concussive wave of heat rippled the underbrush all around them. Kane glanced back and glimpsed fiery debris tumbling from the sky in a flaming rain of destruction.

They had invaded hostile territory and whipped up a recipe for total annihilation with bullets, balls, and blood as the main ingredients. Then they had rammed it down the enemy's throat with a cold steel fist.

But the mission didn't end there. All the death and

destruction didn't matter if they failed to bring Jeremy Reardon home. Ripping the guts out of Sanchez's drug empire was a nice bonus, but it was not the catalyst for this assignment.

Get Jeremy back. That was their objective.

Time to move to target number two—Sanchez's estate.

Time to bring the thunder right to the bastard's door.

CHAPTER 12

Team Reaper Headquarters

Swift drained his fifth cup of coffee, chugging caffeine to stay alert. A direct IV might have been preferable, but with Brick tied up in New York to debrief with the SEALs, there was no medic to hook him up with a needle and a bag of stay-awake juice. So java—lots of java—would have to suffice.

Reynolds was racked out in one of the bunks. No point in both of them staying up. He would roust her if Reaper One called for a drone, but that seemed highly unlikely at this point, given how long it would take to get the Predator UAV over the Colombian jungle. He'd told her to get some shuteye, and she hadn't argued.

So he was all alone when his deep-dive analysis program alerted him that it had dug up a commonality within the data feeds from the terrorist attacks.

He quickly scanned the information, did some double-checking, and confirmed it was legit. He let out a low whistle. "Well, ain't that something," he muttered. The information needed to get to the proper authorities immediately; problem was, Reaper had told him to keep his analyzation of the terrorist attacks on the down-low.

Decisions, decisions.

He dripped Visine into his eyes to moisten away the scratchiness, and by the time the redness started to fade, he knew what he needed to do. Kane was 2,500 kilometers away, quite possibly engaged in a firefight right at this very moment. There was nothing he could do with the information and Swift couldn't afford to sit on it until he got back.

He fired off a silent apology to Reaper and prepared himself for a royal butt-chewing when Thurston found out about his side project. And he would own it, all the way. Getting chewed out never killed anyone. Not a chance in hell would he let her know that Reaper had asked him to look into the terrorist attacks.

Thurston was somewhere on the premises. He normally would have just yelled for her, but he didn't want to wake up Reynolds. So he called her cell phone instead. She answered on the second ring.

"What is it, Slick?" Thurston liked to get straight to the point.

"Got something I need you to see. Something critical."

"From Reaper?"

"It's not about Reaper," Swift replied.

"Then what's it about?"

He hesitated, then sighed and said, "It's about the terrorist attacks."

"That's not..." Her voice trailed off, and Swift heard her match his sigh with one of her own. "I'll be right there."

While he waited for her to appear from wherever she was, Swift queued up some photos. He didn't necessarily need the visual aids to make his report, but it would help.

When Thurston showed up and stood beside his chair, he was ready to roll.

"All right, Slick," she said, her eyes so bleary and blood-shot that he thought about offering her some of his Visine. "What's so important?"

He took a deep breath and said, "I don't think the terrorist attacks are random."

"Why are you looking into the attacks at all? World Wide Drug Initiative, that's what the sign above the door says."

Swift almost pointed out that there was no sign above the door but thought better of it. Somehow, he doubted Thurston was in the mood for smart-aleck comments.

"World Wide Drug Initiative," she repeated. "Four words, and not one of them has anything to do with terrorism."

Swift shrugged. "I've got plenty of downtime while the team runs around shooting people, so I thought I would filter the data through one of my analysis programs."

Thurston folded her arms. She looked like a school-marm getting ready to scold a problematic student. "Reaper put you up to this, right?"

"Negative. This was all my idea."

"You're full of crap, Slick."

"Is that a compliment?"

"Absolutely not. When Reaper gets back, we may need to have a chat about operational protocol during missions."

"I never jeopardized—"

She cut him off. "Just tell me what you found."

"Like I said, the attacks aren't random. In fact, I'd bet my next paycheck they're related to the cartels."

"Trying to justify taking your computer off the reservation?" Thurston asked.

Swift shook his head. "Not at all. Just hear me out." He punched a button, bringing up the first photo. It showed a middle-aged Italian man with slick-backed hair, dressed in a sharp, tailored suit.

Thurston studied the screen. "I don't recognize him."

"No reason you should," Swift said. "Meet Vincent Gianelli, a midlevel mobster with an old-school flair."

"In other words, he's watched *The Godfather* too many times."

"Exactly. Anyway, he and his mistress were on the *Norwegian Gem* when it was attacked and are now confirmed dead. According to reports in the DEA database, Gianelli oversees a significant portion of the coke-trafficking business in the lower Manhattan area."

"I thought the mob didn't mess with drugs."

"Back in the seventies, they didn't," Swift replied. "They stuck to prostitution, gambling, loan sharking, stuff like that. But when the eighties cocaine boom hit, they didn't have much choice but to expand with the times."

"Okay, but I don't get how a dead mobster killed in a terrorist attack links into the cartels."

"You will. Just stay with me." Swift pulled up another photo. This one showed a Russian man who looked to be in his late thirties. One of his eyes drooped badly, making the other eye seem oversized and slightly bulging by comparison. "Kirill 'Popeye' Popov," Swift announced. "Alleged to have ties to the Russian mob. He, his wife, his eleven-year-old daughter, his sister, and two nieces were all aboard the jet that got blown out of the sky at La Guardia."

"Popeye?" Thurston said. "He might be a good for nothing gangster, but that's still pretty cold."

"Hey, I didn't give him the nickname," Swift protested. "That's what it says in the DEA files."

"He's in the DEA database too?"

"The feds suspect he's part of a pipeline, using his private jet to shuttle coke back from the Florida Keys where he picks it up from a Cuban supplier."

The light bulb blazed to life behind Thurston's tired eyes as she started to catch on. "So, two terrorist attacks, two dead drug dealers."

"Now you're getting it."

"Who's next?"

Another tap of a key, another photo. A clean-cut young man, close-cropped black hair, with blue eyes and wide shoulders. All the stats accompanying the picture as well as the words "DEA" emblazoned across the top made it clear this was an official photo.

"Shawn Potter," Swift said. "Gunned down in the Central Park attack, along with his one-month-old daughter."

"A DEA agent." Thurston scanned the information on the screen. "And from the looks of it, a really good one."

"A rising star," Swift agreed. "Potter had only been with the agency for three years and had already racked up an impressive arrest record."

"So, we've got two dead drug dealers and a dead DEA agent who was putting a serious dent in the city's drug trade," Thurston said. "Interesting, but given the high-volume nature of the attacks, it could also just be random coincidence."

"We're not done yet." Swift brought up the next photo, a young Hispanic male. "Meet Alejandro Lopez. Killed in the church bombing. Just so happens he was a local snitch for the DEA."

Thurston pursed her lips and said nothing, but Swift

could tell the gears were turning in her brain as she processed the information.

"And last but not least," he said, keying up the final photo, "we have Santiago Rodriguez." The picture showed an older Hispanic man with gray hair and narrow eyes, wearing a pinstriped suit. "Owns several grocery stores in Manhattan. DEA suspects him of being one of the biggest importers of Mexican cocaine, using his stores as a front, bringing the drugs across the border in produce trucks."

"Let me guess, he died in the fifth attack."

"He was on the bridge when it went down," Swift confirmed.

"So, three drug dealers, a DEA agent, and a snitch," said Thurston. "Five terrorist attacks, five people in the DEA databases end up dead."

"Among thousands of others... but yeah."

"Why would Islamic extremists target people associated with the narcotics trade?" Thurston wondered.

"They wouldn't," Swift replied. "But someone else would."

"So you think somebody gave the terrorists their targets."

"Not just somebody—Miguel Sanchez."

"The same Miguel Sanchez that Reaper is currently hunting in Colombia?"

"That's the one."

Thurston looked thoughtful. "Explain your theory."

"Think about it," Swift said. "All these targets came from the DEA database and it just so happens that our current mission involves the DEA forming an alliance with Sanchez and his cartel cronies."

"How do the terrorists factor in?"

"My guess is that the cartel is funding them in exchange for being able to select the targets. The cartel eliminates their obstacles—competitors, snitches, et cetera—making it easier for them to monopolize the cocaine traffic in NYC and hides the targeted kills behind the smokescreen of the terrorist attacks."

"First the DEA in bed with the cartels, now the cartels in bed with terrorists. I need a new job." Thurston shook her head. "Okay, so how do we prove any of this?"

"Follow the money," Swift replied. "I've already accessed Paul Jacobs' banking records, so we know he's been receiving large sums of money from an offshore account, which we can logically assume is owned by Miguel Sanchez. I'll access Sanchez's account and see where else he's been sending large sums and maybe that will point us in the direction of this Johnny Jihad."

"Are you going to have any problem hacking into an offshore account?"

Swift rolled his eyes. "Please."

Thurston smiled. "Fair enough. You work on that, and I'll call Jones and brief him on this, then I'll let Reaper know we need Sanchez alive if possible."

"Gonna torture the dirtbag for information on Johnny's whereabouts?"

Thurston's smile grew tight and cold. "I prefer to call it doing whatever is necessary to save lives."

"Wasn't an objection," Swift said. "You can yank Sanchez's guts out his asshole for all I care."

"We'll save that for our backup plan," Thurston replied. "Maybe it won't be necessary, as long as those golden fingers of yours can get us the information we need."

Swift pulled his keyboard closer and got ready to go to work. "I'm on it."

The Sanchez estate

Razor found Sanchez in his bedroom, still wrapped in his bathrobe. He hadn't bothered knocking. The news was too important for formalities. "They hit the compound," the enforcer said without preamble. "Lab, warehouse, barracks... all gone. Total loss. This Team Reaper seems to have a scorched earth policy."

Sanchez paced the room, rubbing his face wearily. "They'll come here soon. It's their next logical choice." He looked at Razor. "Double the patrols, then go to the village and promise them a reward for their heads. Any of their heads. Those worthless peasants know the jungle better than we do. Perhaps they can track down these *Americanos*."

"The villagers have no love for you," Razor warned. "They are more apt to help the Americans than kill them. Enemy of my enemy is my friend and all that."

Sanchez smiled coldly. "Then give them a demonstration of what happens to those who give aid to my enemies. As the Americans say, a picture is worth a thousand words. Paint them a picture in blood."

Colombia

Dawn broke as Team Reaper crouched on the slope of a hill overlooking a farming village, hidden by the thick trees and underbrush. They were sweat-soaked and bone-tired, having spent the last several hours trekking seven kilometers from the destroyed compound through the unforgiving jungle. And they still had three more kilometers to go to reach Sanchez's villa. Now that the sun was on its way up, the heat and humidity would only intensify.

Kane sipped tepid water from his canteen as he studied the collection of weather-worn huts and watched chickens scratch in the dirt between ramshackle fences. Sanchez's fortified estate lay to the west. They would skirt the village and continue toward the target. Reaper had no quarrel with the villagers and no reason to advertise their presence.

Shortly after they began their hike from the burning compound, Thurston had called him on the satellite phone and explained Swift's cartel-funded terrorism theory. She told him to take Sanchez alive if possible. Kane had promised to do his best, but deep down he seriously doubted the drug lord would allow himself to be taken into custody.

As he put away his canteen, he heard an engine approaching. A minute later a black Hummer with over-sized tires and a grill guard that looked heavy enough to serve as a medieval battering ram entered the village and skidded to a halt in a cloud of dust. A bald man wearing jungle fatigues exited the vehicle and without preamble grabbed the nearest girl, a slender young thing who couldn't have been more than fourteen. She was carrying a basket of eggs, which fell to the ground as the man snatched her. The cracked shells leaked runny yolks into the dirt.

Kane recognized her abuser from the mission's intel: the psycho named Razor. The man confirmed his identity by whipping out his namesake weapon and laying the wicked edge against the side of the girl's neck. It wouldn't take much movement or pressure to cut her carotid and uncork a whale-spout of arterial blood.

The villagers gathered around the unfolding drama as Razor spoke loudly, his words carrying all the way up to where Team Reaper hid on the hillside.

"Mr. Sanchez sends his greetings!" the cartel cutthroat shouted.

The throng suddenly parted as a hysterical, weeping woman rushed toward the Hummer, wailing and reaching toward the girl in Razor's grasp. She babbled in Spanish and Kane gathered that she was the mother of the girl, begging for her daughter's life. She might as well have begged a hungry jaguar not to kill a crippled monkey.

Razor waited until the wailing woman was almost on top of him, then pivoted slightly and fired a brutal sidekick into her midsection, his boot sinking deep into her abdomen. The quick, merciless strike drove the woman backwards, the air exploding from her lungs. She collapsed on the ground, clutching her stomach and whimpering in pain but still pleading for him to spare her daughter.

Up on the hill, Axe moved up next to Kane. Keeping his voice low, he said, "Reaper, we're not just gonna sit here and do nothing, are we?"

"No, we're not." Kane motioned Cara over, then asked both of them, "Can either of you put a bullet in that bastard from up here with the HK?"

"Why not just go down there and take him?" Cara suggested. "We've got him outnumbered."

"He could cut her throat any second," Kane replied. "Not sure we'd make it down there in time. Besides, as soon as he saw us coming, he'd kill her."

"He's got a point," Axe said. "Cara, you take the shot."

She looked worried. "Can't promise this ends well."

"If we don't do anything, it doesn't end well for that girl," Kane replied. He knew they couldn't just stand by and watch Razor carve open the village girl's windpipe. But the range was nearly three hundred meters, a tough shot with the HK416 carbine. With her M110A sniper system, Cara could have shot a gnat's legs off at that distance; with the HK, there was a 50/50 chance she would hit the girl instead of Razor. But it was a chance that had to be taken because if they sat on their hands, the girl was dead anyway. Cara was capable of tough shots. Kane just hoped she could pull one off now. He didn't want her to live the rest of her life with an innocent girl's death on her conscience.

"There are intruders in the jungle," Razor shouted at the villagers in Spanish. "An American kill-team has come to our country to destroy Mr. Sanchez. If you find these *cabrones,* kill them. Bring us their heads, any of their heads, and you will be rewarded. Fail us, and we will slaughter every one of your wives and daughters, young and old." He paused for a moment to let the threat sink in, then snarled, "Just like this."

His muscles tensed to slash the girl's throat...

...just as Cara sent a single 5.56mm NATO round downrange.

The suppressor did its job, but Razor never would have heard the shot anyway.

You never hear the bullet that kills you.

The slug slammed into Razor's temple with enough force to blow the man's eyes right out of their sockets. He toppled sideways as the round exited the left side of his skull and hit the dirt with his face a mask of blood and gore. The razor lay in the dust, fallen from the spasming hand of its dead master.

The village girl, splattered with sticky bits of Razor's cranial muck, ran into her mother's arms, sobbing in relieved hysterics. She no doubt knew she had been a heartbeat away from a slit throat, only to be saved by an angel with a bullet.

A death angel.

Or rather, a team of them.

All eyes turned to stare as Kane, Cara, Axe, and Ferrero made their way down the hillside and entered the village. They cut imposing figures, decked out in combat gear and carrying submachine guns, and the villagers backed away from them warily.

Kane walked over to the girl and her mother, kneeling in the dirt as they clutched each other. The mother looked up at him, eyes sparkling with tears, and choked out, *"Gracias, senor."* Her eyes flicked to Cara. *"Gracias, senorita."*

Kane acknowledged her heartfelt gratitude with a nod, glad they had saved the girl's life. Glad that a mother did not have to bury her child tonight. Sometimes they had to become savages in order to fight savages. Good deeds like this helped balance out the scales. Helped them keep their humanity intact. Helped keep them above the level of the beasts they hunted.

He and Cara helped the woman to her feet, then joined Axe and Ferrero, who were in the process of requisitioning the Hummer.

"No point in walking when we can ride," Axe said.

"Amen to that," Cara replied. "I call shotgun."

"After the shot you just made," Ferrero said, "you can ride any damn place you please."

Kane climbed into the driver's seat as Axe and Ferrero slid into the back, leaving the passenger seat for Cara. As he started the vehicle, an elderly man approached. Kane lowered the window to hear what he had to say.

"You killed the Razor." The village elder sounded

awestruck as if a miracle had occurred right before his rheumy eyes.

Kane gave him a mirthless grin. "Yeah, I guess you could say he lost his edge."

"Mr. Sanchez, he will punish us."

"Trust me," Kane said. "After today, you're never gonna have to worry about Sanchez ever again."

With that, he punched the gas and rooster tails fanned from beneath the tires as they raced away from the village. There was death behind them and death before them, and Reaper would have it no other way. That was the life they had chosen. They danced with the devil and enjoyed the tune.

Kane pointed the Hummer in the direction of Sanchez's estate, following the rough road that put the vehicle's suspension to the test. They had just saved one child from a grisly fate, but Jeremy Reardon was still in the murderous hands of evil men. Team Reaper would fight to save him until their dying breath.

Or Jeremy's.

———

The Sanchez estate

As the Hummer rounded a bend in the road fifteen minutes later, Miguel Sanchez's luxurious estate loomed into view up ahead, secured behind a high wall with an iron gate, a guard booth tucked just inside to the left. Somewhere beyond those walls—assuming he was still alive—was Jeremy Reardon. But before Reaper could launch a search-and-rescue strike, Kane had to figure out how to get the guard to open the gate.

Turned out the gods of war were smiling down on them for a change. The guard opened the gate as soon as he saw the Hummer, mistakenly assuming Razor had returned. Complacency combined with sloppiness allowed Kane to just roll on in.

"Easiest target penetration *ever*," Axe said.

"Thought studs like you appreciated easy penetration," Cara wisecracked.

"Well, now that we've penetrated, let's get down to business."

"Working on it," Kane replied, drawing his Sig. Time to punish the sentry for his error.

There was just one guard. He stepped out of the booth as the Hummer rolled up. Kane lowered the tinted window, and before the man could react to the abrupt realization that it wasn't Razor behind the wheel, Kane shot him point-blank in the face. Blood splattered the guardhouse as the corpse toppled to the ground with everything below his nose mangled into red mush. The cartel might cover the funeral but it for damn sure would be closed casket.

One down, only God knew how many more to go.

Time to kick the bloodbath into high gear.

There were coke-slinging, kid-stealing dirtbags who needed to die.

No point in keeping them waiting.

"Buckle up," Kane rasped. He aimed the Hummer at the front door of the mansion and stomped on the gas. Shredded turf erupted from beneath the tires as the vehicle surged forward.

The sudden rev of the engine alerted nearby soldiers. As the speeding vehicle tore across the immaculately land-scaped lawn and roared up the front steps of the villa, they peppered the Hummer with bullets. Kane heard the *thwack-thwack-thwack* of slugs tattooing the metalwork and flinched as a round nicked his ear.

The stone steps acted as a ramp and launched the Hummer into the air like a two-ton missile. Glass and wood exploded in all directions as the vehicle jumped right through the front walls of the mansion. A thick cloud of dust and debris roiled into the air.

The Reaper warriors wasted no time. They immediately exited the crashed Hummer, glass crunching under their boots, and whipped their HK416s into play.

A cartel soldier materialized through the dusty haze and Kane immediately dispatched him with a quick burst that vaporized everything above his eyebrows. Before the dead guy even hit the floor, they were on the move, carbines tight to shoulders, seeking more targets.

A spiral staircase twisted its way up to the second floor of the villa. A guard appeared on the upper landing, leaning over the railing with an AK-47. Ferrero fired first, chopping ragged holes in the man's torso with a six-round salvo. The soldier jerked and twitched in a spastic death-dance and then toppled over the railing, his short dive ending in a wet crunch as he face-planted on the tile floor.

"On me!" Kane commanded, racing up the stairs. He didn't look back to see if the others were behind him. They would follow him right to the gates of Hell if that's where he led them.

As he hit the landing, he spotted a single door to his right. He also spotted a guard posted outside the door, clamping down on the trigger of his AK. The sentry missed the mark, bullets flying wide to chew into the wall. Kane punished the man's poor marksmanship with a burst to the guts that tracked upward to unzip the sentry from navel to neck. The man went down with the life ripped right out of him.

Kane stepped over the corpse with less thought than he would have given a swatted fly and kicked in the door. They entered the master bedroom in combat crouches, Cara swinging right while Axe went left. Ferrero turned and took a knee in the doorway, facing the hallway, ready to defend their six.

Some part of Kane's brain subconsciously noted the opulent luxury of the room, but his warrior mind focused on Miguel Sanchez and Jeremy Reardon. He had come here to rescue a kid, not admire the drapes.

The drug lord had Jeremy standing on the edge of a king-sized waterbed, using him as a shield as he kept a stainless-steel Smith & Wesson .357 Magnum pressed against the kid's temple.

"Hiding behind a little kid," Kane said. "Just like the gutless coward you are."

"Sticks and stones and all that *mierda*," Sanchez sneered. "Drop your guns or—"

"Yeah, yeah, I know," Reaper interrupted. "Or you'll blow his brains out. I've heard it all before."

"Whatever you're gonna do, Reaper, do it fast," Axe urged. "We don't have time to jerk around."

Kane noted the hammer on Sanchez's double-action revolver wasn't cocked, meaning it would take nearly ten pounds of pressure to fire the revolver and put a bullet through Jeremy's brain. A mistake on Sanchez's part, because if Kane could find a way to get a kill-shot into the drug lord, his death spasms wouldn't generate enough force to fire the Magnum.

Kane could see a small section of Sanchez's face as the

drug lord peered around Jeremy's head, his right eye visible just above the top of the kid's earlobe. A tempting target, but if he was even slightly off, he would shoot an innocent boy in the face. But if he didn't find a way to kill Sanchez fast, the room would be swarmed with guards, and it would be game over.

As if to confirm the urgency, Cara hissed, "Reaper, we've gotta do something right now, or we're dead meat."

Jeremy stood frozen on the bed, not daring to struggle or squirm with the muzzle of the .357 Magnum tucked tight to his temple. He looked at Kane with fear in his eyes and mouthed the words, *Help me, mister.*

"I'll kill him!" Sanchez warned. His gun-hand remained rock steady. Clearly, the drug lord was no stranger to tense, violent situations.

"You've got one chance to put down the gun, give me the boy, and walk out of here alive," Kane growled, knowing the numbers were running down fast. "Because I'm not walking out of here without the kid."

"You're not walking out of here at all," Sanchez retorted. "My men will be here any second and cut you all to pieces."

"Guess that means I don't have much time. Last chance, asshole. Put down the gun."

"Or what?"

Kane bared his teeth in a wolfish smile. Enough of this bullshit. He had learned long ago that when you only had one option, you took it. He surreptitiously used his thumb to flick the HK's fire selector switch to semi-automatic mode. "Or I'll kill you."

"Ha!" Sanchez mocked. "How do you plan on pulling that trick off?"

"Glad you asked."

Kane hit the trigger.

Jeremy Reardon flinched as the bullet split the top of his ear.

Miguel Sanchez did a whole lot more than flinch as the slug passed through Jeremy's ear and drilled a hole in the drug lord's face right below his eye. The 5.56mm death-dealer tore a devastating channel through his head until it slammed against the rear skull-bone and exited in a bloody burst of brain matter.

The impact punched Sanchez backwards like he had been walloped by a wrecking ball. The unfired .357 fell from his hands as he bounced off the wall and slid to the floor, what remained of his face slackening in death.

Jeremy fell onto the bed, crying out in pain and clutching at his bloody ear. His eyes were saucer-wide and full of tears. "You shot me, mister!"

"Yeah," Kane said. "Sometimes you gotta lose some skin to save your ass."

"We've got company!" Ferrero announced. "The welcome party has arrived."

Kane heard enemy boots pounding up the spiral staircase. Time to get the hell out of here.

He pulled the pin on a fragmentation grenade as he moved toward the door, holding it in his right fist while he hefted the HK in his left. The Sig still rode in its holster as backup if the time came. Or more likely, *when* the time came. Because Kane had no doubt that if they wanted to have any chance of getting out alive, they would need to unleash every bullet they had.

Unleash their inner savagery.

No quarter. No mercy.

The only way to play this game.

Ferrero opened fire as Kane leaned out and tossed the fragger down the hall. The lead soldier went down with

Ferrero's burst drilling his chest. The grenade bounced off the body and ricocheted toward the next guy in line. The gunman scrambled backwards, crashing into his comrades behind him, creating a domino effect. They tried to retreat in a cursing, yelling, panicking melee of flailing limbs. Then the grenade detonated and turned them into a dying, moaning, screaming mess of shredded meat.

"Stay close," Kane said to Jeremy. He patted Ferrero on the shoulder, and they all moved out of the bedroom, he and Ferrero rapid-walking down the hall side by side, with Axe and Cara bringing up the rear. Jeremy stayed glued to his six like a shadow.

They slipped through the slick swath of blood and guts spread everywhere and started down the spiral staircase, but a burst of auto-fire from below forced them to pull back. Splinters chipped from the railing, and a ricocheting slug grazed Jeremy's side, causing him to cry out in pain.

Kane plucked another grenade from his webbing and tossed it over the rail, down into the cluster of enemy gunners. The explosion decimated them, pulpy red chunks flying everywhere. A blown-off head tumbled across the floor like a lumpy bowling ball and came to a stop at the base of the stairs.

Kane quickly checked the boy's wound. Superficial, nothing more. The bullet had merely grazed him, peeling off a strip of flesh and leaving behind a bloody trench. To a ten-year-old kid, it probably hurt like crazy, but he would have to suck it up. "You'll live," he said. *Well, maybe,* he silently added, turning his full attention back to the lethal task of getting them out of here alive.

More troops poured into the mansion through the hole in the wall created by the crashing Hummer. Kane knew it was now or never. "All right, boys and girls," he said into his com. "Time to shoot some motherfuckers."

"Rock 'n' roll," Axe snarled. "Hell, yeah!"

Kane plucked a pair of flashbangs from his webbing and tossed them over the railing. As soon as the grenades detonated with their 180-decibel thunder and one million candela blast of blinding light, the team was on the move, racing down the stairs while the soldiers below were deaf, blind, and incapacitated.

As soon as Kane's boots touched down on the main floor, his HK hunted for targets. The debilitating effects of a flashbang could last as little as five seconds, and he wanted to make sure the threats were put down before they regained their senses.

Adrenalin burned through his veins as Kane cut loose with the carbine and sent 5.56mm hornets buzzing toward the soldiers staggering around the Hummer with blood trickling from their ear canals. The guns of Axe, Ferrero, and Cara joined him a half-second later.

Dozens of red-hot projectiles nailed the cartel henchmen where they stood, scything through their bodies and sending them to meet their Maker. The twitching, shuddering corpses bounced off the Hummer like epileptic victims and corkscrewed to the ground in scarlet sprays.

More soldiers appeared, and Kane kept his finger on the trigger, tearing them apart. The others followed suit, taking on targets as they rushed toward their position. They didn't make every shot count—damn near impossible on full-auto —but they didn't miss much either. Bullets drilled into bad guys, and a bloody haze filled the air. Living enemies turned into dead enemies, just the way Reaper liked them.

Kill 'em all. Right now it was their only chance.

Kane swapped magazines and, with a scared-to-death

Jeremy sticking close, led the way through the carnage. The sharp, acidic stench of death bit into his nostrils. Over in the corner, a dying-but-not-quite-dead-yet soldier screamed in pain, trembling fingers clutching at a belly wound. Kane expended a bullet to end the man's misery.

As the team moved outside, they found more enemy troops out on the front lawn scurrying about like confused beetles. Clearly, Sanchez had put his faith in the quantity of his soldiers rather than the quality. A mistake that cost him his life—and would cost them theirs.

All four Reaper warriors opened fire and saturated the kill-zone with hot slugs, sending the enemy soldiers to eternal damnation one by one.

The HK416s ripped the targets to bits as they were caught in a crisscross cyclone of lethal lead. Blood sprayed from bullet-torn flesh as men dropped, dead or dying, blown to gibbets by Team Reaper's full-auto hellstorm.

Kane performed another magazine exchange. The others followed suit. Jeremy watched them, one hand pressed to his clipped ear, the other holding his scorched ribs. With their weapons topped off, the team did a quick search for survivors, heads on swivels. They found one in the garage—the last man standing, as it were—and Kane smoked him. The burst of auto-fire slashed across his chest in spurts of red and he crashed to the ground, leaving the Sanchez estate undefended.

Kane sent Cara and Ferrero back inside to collect all the cell phones, computers, and files they could find. Axe helped himself to a Land Rover sitting in the garage, tucking Jeremy inside while he checked out the engine. Meanwhile, Kane fired up the sat-phone to give Thurston the news.

She answered on the first ring, which let him know she'd been waiting for the call. "Thurston."

Since she didn't waste any time with preambles, neither did Kane. "It's Reaper," he said. "You want the good news or the bad news?"

"I could use some good news right about now."

"We have Jeremy Reardon."

He heard her sigh in relief. "My God, that *is* good news. I'll notify Traynor." She paused, then asked, "Okay, what's the bad news?"

"Sanchez is dead."

Silence for a moment, followed by, "Did it have to be done?"

"If you wanted the boy alive, yeah."

"Then I'm good with it."

That surprised Kane. "Really? Thought you'd be pissed."

"A young boy is alive, and a drug lord is dead," Thurston said. "I call that an acceptable outcome. God knows it could have been a lot worse."

"What about Sanchez's connection to the terrorists?"

"Slick managed to hack into his offshore accounts. I'll spare you all the technical details, but he was able to follow the money trail—just under three million—to a shell corporation in New York City. He managed to dig up the name and address of the guy behind the shell. If we're right, he's living on a houseboat in New Jersey."

"You think it's Johnny?"

"That's what we're betting on."

"I'd love to go knock on his door, but we're a long way from home."

"Brick and Traynor are still in New York. They can handle it."

"Traynor may not be willing to walk away from Reardon," Kane reminded her.

"If he won't leave his buddy to stop the mastermind behind five terror attacks on U.S. soil that resulted in thousands of deaths, you won't have to fire him because I'll do it myself," Thurston replied with a sharp edge to her voice.

"Copy that," he said. "We'll wrap things up here and head for home."

"Safe travels. See you on the other side."

Kane hung up as Cara and Ferrero returned with a satchel full of laptops and cell phones. Slick would have a field day cracking all their electronic secrets. There was a good chance that those devices contained the intel that would lead to their next assignment. Because this war never ended. But they needed to exfil from this mission before they could worry about the next one.

Axe closed the hood and gave him a thumbs up. "She's got gas and oil, so we're good to go."

"Perfect," Kane said. "This place sucks. Let's go home."

CHAPTER 13

Angel of Mercy Hospital
New York City

Traynor sat in the chair next to Mike Reardon's hospital bed, flipping through an entertainment magazine he'd found in the bottom drawer of the nightstand. It was so old there was an article covering the wedding of Brad Pitt and Jennifer Aniston.

An NYPD police officer who barely looked old enough to shave was stationed out in the hall, the first line of defense if Omega showed up to finish the job. If that happened, Traynor had no doubt that the assassin would go through the cop like a lion going through a lamb. But no way on God's green earth would the killer get through him.

Reardon was sleeping, momentarily free from the pain of his wounds thanks to a morphine drip. He surfaced from the narcotic fog periodically, and the first thing he always asked was, "Did they find Jeremy yet?" It hurt Traynor's heart every time he had to shake his head and tell his friend no.

His cell phone vibrated, the screen lighting up in the dimness of the room. He looked at the number and saw that it was headquarters calling. He swallowed hard, wondering if this was the call he had been dreading, the call where Thurston told him to not bother coming back.

He walked over to the window that looked out on the city, down at the roads that were usually filling up with traffic at this time of the morning. Today they were mostly barren due to the threat of another terror attack. Keeping his voice low to avoid waking Reardon, he pressed the button to answer the call. "Traynor."

"It's Thurston," the general said. "We need to talk."

Traynor sighed. "Yeah, I figured this was coming. Just thought Reaper would at least do it face to face."

"Reaper is in Colombia, remember?"

"Yeah, I remember."

"And this can't wait," Thurston said.

"Yeah, I get it."

"How's Reardon?"

Traynor glanced over his shoulder at his sleeping friend. "He was kneecapped and cut to ribbons, but he's hanging in there. He's tough. He's asleep right now, so I guess this is as good a time as any to have this conversation."

"Well, when he wakes up," Thurston said, "you can give him some good news."

"What's that?"

"They got his boy."

So much relief rushed through him that he nearly dropped the phone. He fumbled it back to his ear and said, "Are you serious? Tell me you're serious."

"I'm serious," Thurston said. "They found him at Sanchez's estate."

"Is he okay?"

"Missing a chunk of his ear and a bullet grazed his ribs, but he's fine."

"Thank God."

"Thank God if you want, just don't forget to thank your teammates when you see them again."

She means 'if' I see them again, Traynor thought to himself. Aloud he asked, "What about Sanchez? Dead or alive?"

"Dead."

"Who did it?"

"You can let Reardon know that Reaper put a bullet in the face of the man who took his son and ordered his wife killed."

"He'll be happy to hear that."

"Now for the bad news," Thurston said, not bothering with a smooth segue.

Traynor took a deep breath, then slowly exhaled. "I'm ready," he said, steeling himself for the dreaded words that would see him terminated from Team Reaper.

"I need you on a mission."

That was *not* what he had expected to hear. "Can you repeat that?"

Thurston quickly brought him up to speed, including Sanchez's suspected connection with the terrorists, then said, "We think Johnny Jihad is holed up on a houseboat over in New Jersey. Slick is sending the intel to your phone as we speak. Rendezvous with Brick at JFK. I'll arrange for a chopper to get you to New Jersey ASAP so you can go find this son of a bitch."

"Are you sure about this?" Traynor asked. "Me and Reaper, we didn't exactly part on the best of terms."

"I'm aware," Thurston replied. "But unless you know something I don't, Reaper hasn't actually fired you yet, so for now you are still a part of this team, which means I can still activate you. But if you want to keep babysitting, just say the word."

Traynor knew he didn't have a choice. It had nothing to do with Team Reaper. It had to do with who he was as a man. As a *warrior*. Johnny Jihad had slaughtered thousands of people in just two short days. He had to be stopped, crushed like a bug, and Traynor had just been asked to do the stomping. He couldn't say no. So instead he said, "I'll be there."

"Good man," Thurston said. "You need to get moving, and I mean right now. Johnny threatened another attack today so every second counts."

"Copy that," he said. "And General?"

"Yes?"

"Thanks." He left it at that.

She didn't. "The prodigal son returns," she said, her voice a bit softer than usual. "Welcome home and happy hunting."

Traynor quickly wrote a note for Reardon. He kept it vague, knowing a nurse or doctor might see it first, but Mike would be able to read between the lines and understand why he had to go. He knew his friend wouldn't hold it against him because Reardon wasn't that kind of man. Traynor set the note on the nightstand and gently patted Reardon's shoulder. "Gotta take care of some business, Mike. I'll be back before you know it."

He left the room with a brisk stride and a grim set to his jaw, a gun-slinging crusader ready to crush an unholy jihad.

Here I come, Johnny-boy.

———

Colombia

The exfiltration from Sanchez's villa back to the SOC-R proved uneventful. They left the Land Rover near the smoldering remains of the processing plant and hiked the rest of the way to the boat. The journey back upriver went off without a hitch as well.

Axe patted the minigun the way someone would pat a loyal dog, a look of regret on his face. "With this much firepower to play with, it's almost a shame we didn't get to use it."

"Enjoy the easy times," Ferrero said. "God knows we don't get many of 'em."

"Ain't that the fucking truth," Cara muttered.

"Language," Ferrero scolded. "We've got a kid with us."

"Yeah," Kane grinned. "You'd think a mom would know better."

Cara smiled back, but Kane caught the flicker of pain just beneath the surface and knew she was thinking about her son Jimmy. Cara was born for combat, never more fully alive than when she faced down death, but she missed her boy. Team Reaper kept her busy, which meant she didn't get a chance to visit him as often as she would like, and Kane knew that sometimes she struggled with guilt. Truth was, he knew exactly how she felt. His sister Melanie might be in a coma, but he knew he should still visit her more often. Maybe when this mission was all wrapped up, he and Cara could take a road trip to visit their loved ones.

"It's okay, ma'am," Jeremy reassured her. "I've heard f-bombs before." He lowered his voice to a conspiratorial whisper as if the jungle had ears and he didn't want it to hear what he was about to say. "Once, I even called a bully at school a fucking peckerhead right before I kicked him in the privates. But don't tell my dad."

They all enjoyed a good laugh and Axe said, "Don't worry, kid, your secret's safe with us."

But when the laughter died, Kane had a sobering thought—the poor kid didn't know his mother was gone. Didn't know that her loving arms wouldn't be there to welcome him when he got home. And it wasn't their place to tell him. He had survived one hell, but he still had one more to go through.

It made Kane wish he could bring Sanchez back from the dead just so he could kill him all over again.

The rest of the boat ride passed in silence save for the thrum of the engine. They beached the SOC-R at the trail to the airstrip, then Kane toggled his com. "Reaper Three, Bravo Three. This is Reaper One. Copy?"

It took a minute, but Teller's voice came through. "Bravo Three to Reaper One, we copy. Be advised, we have relocated to the hangar."

"Copy that, Bravo Three."

"Do you have the package?"

"Ten-four. A little banged up, but otherwise safe and sound."

"Glad to hear it. Casualties?"

"Negative."

"Copy that. See you in a few. Bravo Three out."

They double-timed it back to the hangar and found Arenas propped up on an old sofa while Teller and Oswald sat at a rickety table. Somewhere a generator was running, and strategically-placed fans tried—and mostly failed—to take the edge off the already oppressive mid-morning heat.

Oswald treated them to an ear-to-ear grin. He looked genuinely glad to see them. "Well, I'll be buggered, but I really didn't expect all you blokes to make it back in one piece."

"Sorry to disappoint you," Kane said.

"Oh, don't be a tool, mate. Just 'cause I didn't expect it doesn't mean I ain't happy it went down that way." Oswald jerked his chin toward Jeremy. "Looks like you got what you came for."

"Sure did."

The Aussie mercenary gestured toward Arenas. "Heard all the shooting after you left, so I took a stroll to check it out and found your boys." He pointed at Teller. "That big bruiser nearly blew my head off with his twitchy trigger finger."

"Make some damn noise next time, for god's sake," Teller snapped. He looked at Kane. "The guy's quieter than a barefoot Apache walking on cotton."

"Anyway," Oswald said, ignoring Teller's complaint, "I figured they'd be more comfortable waiting for you here than hanging out under a tree waiting for a monkey to crap on their noggins." He slapped Kane on the shoulder. "No extra charge, mate."

"Appreciate that," Kane said. "Now if you don't mind, I've got an injured man to get to the hospital and a little boy to get back to his father, so I'd like to be wheels-up ASAP."

"Roger that," the pilot said. He spun on his heel and exited the hangar to make pre-flight preparations.

Twenty minutes later they were airborne and heading home. Kane felt the weariness sink into his bones. As he watched the jungle canopy whisk by beneath them, Kane silently hoped he never had to come back to Colombia.

He also knew that particular hope was a waste of time.

For every Sanchez they put down for a dirt nap, another one sprang up to take his place and fill in the void. The tentacles of the narcotics hydra were legion; you could spend your whole life chopping them off and never run out of targets. The best they could hope for was to keep wounding the beast and make it bleed.

Blood and thunder, hell yeah.

That was the Reaper way.

CHAPTER 14

New Jersey

The terrorist mastermind known to the world as Johnny Jihad lived in a houseboat on the Hudson River at a marina in northern New Jersey. Not a chintzy houseboat either, Traynor saw. Looked like some of the $3 million the cartel had funneled to the rebirthed Al-Qaeda cell had been used to set up their leader quite nicely. No living in squalor, sacrificing wealth and comfort for the cause. Not for Johnny boy.

Then again, maybe the houseboat hadn't been purchased with drug money. Maybe Johnny had a lucrative side business writing unicorn-on-sasquatch BDSM erotica under a pen name. Wherever the funding had originated, the boat clearly had cost some serious cash.

Traynor wondered if the insurance covered bullet holes.

The strike would have been easier under the cover of darkness instead of the sunny glare of late morning, but they couldn't wait for nightfall while the most wanted terrorist on the planet sat in his houseboat and plotted more destruction. He had to be taken down, and it had to happen now.

Traynor and Brick had briefly considered an underwater assault, using scuba gear to approach the boat from below, but had discarded the idea in favor of a faster, more direct approach.

They went undercover.

Instead of fatigues, combat boots, and tactical vests, they donned cargo shorts, sneakers, and loose, untucked, button-down shirts. They blended right in with all the other boat owners walking around the marina, and the baggy shirts helped hide the suppressed Sig M17s riding in hip holsters.

As they strolled down the docks, drawing nearer to Johnny's boat, Traynor noted the bodyguards on the upper deck of the vessel. Granted, they didn't look like sentries, but that's exactly what they were. They watched everything a little too closely and their hands never strayed far from their waistbands, where you could detect the tell-tale bulge of a pistol if you knew what to look for.

Brick and Traynor knew what to look for.

"Shit," Brick muttered as they walked. "We've got to take out those guards."

"Wonderful," Traynor said. "We're about to start a firefight at a public marina in the middle of the damn day."

"Want to abort?"

"Not an option," Traynor replied. "This guy has already killed thousands, and he's promised to kill even more today."

"His dogs open fire, some innocents might die."

"If we walk away, lots of innocents might die."

"Rock and a hard place, man."

"You know it," Traynor said. "So, let's get it done."

He hated the thought of innocent civilians getting

caught in the crossfire, but there was no other way. He just hoped God, luck, fate, or whatever you wanted to call it was on their side today.

As for the guards, they were protecting the man pulling the strings on mass murder. As far as Traynor was concerned, they were guilty as sin. Which meant him and Brick would be going with the lethal option. Put 'em down for the count and make sure they stayed there.

They brazenly strolled down the dock which led to Johnny's houseboat. They banked on the fact that the guards would be reluctant to engage and bring attention to the fact that the most wanted man in the world was hunkered below deck. The guards would let them get too close, at which time Traynor and Brick would make them pay for their mistake.

As they approached, the sentries eyed them with hard stares. As they drew alongside the boat, one of the men leaned over the railing and waved them off. "Hey, this isn't a tourist attraction. Drag your asses somewhere else before I come down there and make you."

What an idiot, Traynor thought. The guy should have been pulling his pistol and filling them full of holes, not flapping his gums with smack-talk like a high-school locker room. Johnny might have bought himself a really nice boat, but he should have skimped on some upgrades and hired some better security specialists instead.

Traynor flipped back his shirt, drew his Sig, and fired with a speed that caught the sentry completely off guard. The guy didn't even make a move toward his pistol before the 9mm slug ripped into his neck. The sentry staggered back, blood spraying from a clipped artery. His brain finally got the message that he was dead and dumped him on the deck.

Peters took out the second guard, putting a bullet under the target's jaw that burrowed up into his brain and killed him instantly.

Then the whole thing went right to hell.

Another guard materialized on the upper deck. But unlike the first two, this one was more than ready to fight and didn't care how much noise he made. He leaned over the polished brass railing and cut loose with an Ingram MAC-10, spraying a stream of .45 caliber slugs. The sub-gun sported no suppressor, so the crackling *brrrrrppp!* of the full-auto fusillade reverberated across the marina waters. People who had been standing on the docks or on their boats now frantically dove for cover. At least two people leaped into the river with cries of alarm and loud splashes. There were screams, but they were overpowered by the MAC-10's *rat-a-tat-tat* roar.

Traynor and Brick threw themselves onto the boat and rolled, evading the tracking line of auto-fire that pounded the deck just inches from their vulnerable flesh. Splinters exploded into the air all around them.

Johnny Jackass knows we're here now, Traynor thought as his survival instincts kicked into high gear. He kept a tight grip on his gun as he rolled. He had no doubt Brick was doing the same. They both knew the MAC-10 would burn through its magazine in a few short seconds. They just had to dodge the bullets for another heartbeat.

The gunfire abruptly ceased as the sentry's weapon ran dry. Traynor and Brick halted their rolls at the same time, stopping on their backs with the Sigs filling their fists. The sentry tried to pull back from the railing but was a half-second too late. The pistols bucked. Brick's bullet bounced off the brass railing. Traynor's shot blew the man's face off.

He flipped backward and crashed down in a twitching pile of blood-splattered death.

The Reaper warriors climbed to their feet and moved toward the wheelhouse. Another guard appeared, and a fresh line of auto-fire sizzled toward them. Traynor winced as a bullet scorched a raw trench across his ribs and put holes in a perfectly good shirt. The sudden flare of pain fueled his fury. He whipped up his Sig, but Brick had already punched the man a one-way ticket to hell, putting a round through his right eyeball. The guard corkscrewed to the ground.

Traynor almost put another bullet in the corpse for good measure but decided that would be unprofessional. That didn't stop him from giving the dead guy a good kick in the ribs when he walked by though.

Guards neutralized, Traynor and Brick descended below deck, hunting for Johnny. They kept their fingers tight on the triggers, ready to turn the terrorist into maggot food. They usually took no particular pleasure in their kills, but this time they might make an exception.

Senses taut, ready to unleash violence, they edged down a narrow passageway. To the right was a kitchenette; to the left, a bathroom. Which meant the door at the end of the passage must lead to the bedroom. Assuming he hadn't already rabbited, that was where they expected to find their prey.

In the lead, Traynor reached the door first. Brick hugged the bulkhead to the left and nodded to signal he was ready.

Traynor delivered a powerful kick that smashed the door open like balsa wood. He immediately saw Johnny Jihad standing at the back of the bedroom, legs spread wide in an almost comically exaggerated action pose. The terrorist had an RPG-7 raised, the back-blast scorching the wall behind him as he sent the warhead rocketing toward the intruders.

An RPG? Traynor thought. Are you kidding me?

He heard Johnny screaming something about death to infidels, but he was too busy shouting, "Get down!" as he shoved Brick into the bathroom nook.

The grenade sizzled past his head, close enough for him to hear the fin stabilizers pop open. He threw himself in the opposite direction, toward Johnny, as the grenade slammed into the stairs at the far end of the hallway and detonated on impact.

As he landed on his chest, the shockwave from the blast propelled him into a power-skid across the floor. He rolled onto his back as he slid to a halt right between Johnny's spread feet.

Before the Bin Laden-wannabe could leap away, Traynor jammed the muzzle of the Sig right up between Johnny's legs and started pulling the trigger as fast as possible. Blood spurted all over him as he dumped half a magazine at point blank range. The bullets shattered bone and ripped up through Johnny's guts.

With his groin shot to shit, the terrorist mastermind crashed to the floor. Traynor managed to roll out of the way just before getting crushed beneath the mortally wounded man.

The boat started to cant. The grenade had blown a hole in the hull and water poured in.

Brick emerged from the bathroom. "Holy crap!" he exclaimed. "Was that an RPG?"

Traynor fixed a cold stare on the terrorist. Johnny shuddered in pain, eyes burning with both hate and agony. "I need to know where the next attack is," Traynor said. "Tell me that, and I'll end your pain. If not, you can sit there and think about dying hard and slow."

Johnny's face twisted into a snarl. "Allah will save me."

"Oh yeah?" Traynor waved the Sig in front of the man's face. "Where was Allah when I was blowing your balls off, huh?"

"You will die for your blasphemy."

"Maybe, but you get to go first."

Traynor glanced around the room, shifting his balance to compensate for the slowly-tilting deck. To his right hung the slashed, blood-splattered American flag Johnny had used in all his videos. He went over and ripped it down. On the wall behind it was a white dry-erase board. It only had six things written on it.

Ship

Jet

Park

Church

Bridge

1 PP

He looked at the last line and felt a cold chill shiver down his backbone.

He muttered a curse as he went back over to the gut-shot terrorist. Stepping close, he pressed the tip of the Sig's suppressor to the bridge of Johnny's nose. "Different question, same offer," he said. "Tell me about the attack on One Police Plaza."

Johnny just smiled at him with chattering, blood-flecked teeth.

The deck shifted again.

"Just smoke the son of a bitch and let's get out of here," Brick urged. "This boat is going down fast."

"We need information," Traynor said. "We have to stop the attack."

"You will get nothing from me," Johnny vowed. "And you will stop nothing."

"See?" Brick said. "He ain't gonna tell you jack."

It was true, Traynor realized. Johnny's bowels had been blown apart, and shock had already begun to numb his pain. The man was a zealot, perfectly willing to die for his cause and become a martyr. Nothing else Traynor could do to him would overcome that. Johnny Jihad would rather suffer a slow, agonizing death than tell them how to stop the attack on One Police Plaza.

Enough screwing around, Traynor decided.

"You know what? You're right," he rasped. "*Allahu Akbar*, asshole." He pulled the trigger and put a bullet between Johnny's eyes, blowing his brains out all over the scorched wall behind him. From houseboat to hell in a single heartbeat.

"Grab everything you can," Traynor said to Brick, "and let's get out of here."

"Now you're talking."

As Brick gathered up evidence, Traynor pulled out his cell phone and snapped a photo of the dead terrorist. Much like Bin Laden's much-ballyhooed killing, Traynor seriously doubted the public would ever actually see the corpse of Johnny Jihad, but he knew the President would require proof before he announced to America that the terrorist was dead. He sent the photo to headquarters. They would get it where it needed to go.

He slid the phone into his pocket and turned to see Brick staring at some documents. "What's the matter?"

"Shit," Brick said. "I think I know how the strike on One Police Plaza is going down."

Traynor took a look. "Yeah, I'd say 'shit' about covers it. Let's get out of here. We need to call Thurston ASAP."

Traynor was glad their phones were waterproof, because with the stern of the boat now underwater, they were going to have to swim to get off the sinking vessel.

As he and Brick climbed out of the river and up onto the dock, Brick said, "The guy had an RPG, man. What the hell is a terrorist doing with an RPG on a damn houseboat?"

Traynor saw people staring at them from a distance. Trying to act nonchalant was a waste of time, given that they had just emerged dripping wet from a sinking boat that had been the scene of a gunfight and an explosion.

"Who knows?" Traynor said. "Maybe he was worried about Somalian pirates or something."

"We're in New Jersey, not Somalia."

"Not a whole lot of difference."

"We're gonna go viral." Brick pointed at the rubber-neckers who had their phones out, recording for imminent YouTube uploads.

"Everyone gets their fifteen minutes," Traynor said. "Maybe it's just our turn."

"We're a covert task force," Brick replied. "The morning news is not where they want our ugly mugs."

"Nothing we can do about it," Traynor said. "Besides, who you calling ugly? I consider myself to be rather dashing." He shook the water off his phone and called HQ.

Brooklyn, New York

Ken Liddleman—dubbed "Little Man" by his patrol partner, thanks to the unfortunate combination of his last name and below-average height of just five foot three—had been policing the streets of New York City for nearly eleven years now. His partner, Monty Preston, had been on the beat for just under ten years. In their two decades of combined experience, they had seen things they would never forget.

They had been paired up for the last four years, starting out on the zombie shift before making the move to days a year ago. Neither of them missed working nights. Sure, bad stuff happened during the daylight hours, but there was more nightmare fuel once the sun went down.

Ken took a long gulp of coffee—sugar, no cream—and let out a long, tired sigh, hoping the caffeine would combat his weariness. Next to him, Monty chugged down a Red Bull for the same reason. They had been working damn near around the clock since the terrorist attacks and sleep deprivation was starting to take its toll.

As if on cue, Monty let out a jaw-stretching yawn. "Oh, man," he said, shaking his head to clear away the fog. "I want my wife for, like, two minutes, and then I want to hit the sack for at least twelve hours."

Ken yawned in sympathy. "Yeah, that sounds like a plan."

Monty feigned indignation. "Did you just say you want my wife?"

Ken chuckled. "Nah, man, I'm too tired to give it to your wife. I'll settle for the sleep."

"So now Rachel's not good enough for you? Screw you, Little Man."

Ken chuckled again. "Monty, no girl wants to be with a guy called 'Little Man,' if you catch my drift.'

"Rachel says size doesn't matter."

"That's what all the girls say to the guys with small dicks."

They were parked just off the Brooklyn Bridge approach ramp on the Brooklyn side, taking a break. With a lot of businesses shuttered due to the terror attacks, looting was a major problem. They had made three arrests already today. Now, with shift change just an hour away, it was time to kick back and catch a breather. They would have eight hours off to see their families, grab some sleep, and be back in at midnight to pull another double.

"How's the baby doing?" Ken asked. Monty had a four-month-old daughter.

"Good," his partner replied. "Though at the rate we're going, by the time I see her again, she'll probably be graduating from college."

"Well, look on the bright side, with all the mandatory OT we're raking in, you'll be able to afford her wedding pretty soon."

Monty set his can of Red Bull up on the dash and pointed at two men crossing the street toward them. "Heads up. Looks like company coming."

Ken turned and studied the pair as they approached. Young men, early to mid-twenties, wearing dress jeans and casual sports coats. Probably worked for one of those hip new companies that had a relaxed, modernized version of casual business attire. They both smiled as they walked up to the patrol car. One of them tapped on the window.

Ken rolled the window down halfway. "Howdy, folks. What can we do for you?"

"Hello," the man said. "My name is Paul." He gestured toward his companion, who stood just behind him, hands in the pockets of his sports jacket. "That's Rick. We're trying to find One Police Plaza and were hoping you could help us out."

"Sure, no problem." Ken pointed at the approach ramp. "Take the bridge. It's a little over a mile walk."

"A mile?" Paul seemed surprised. "Bit far, huh?"

"Little bit," Ken agreed. "But not too bad."

"Any chance you could give us a ride?"

Ken turned and gave Monty a look, eyebrows raised. You didn't hear that question every day. Chuckling, he turned back to Paul. "Sorry, fella, but we're a patrol car, not an Uber."

Paul's smile never wavered. "Sure, I understand. Sorry."

"No need to apologize."

"Oh, but there is." Paul stepped aside as Rick whipped a .22 semi-automatic pistol from his coat pocket and put two rounds into Ken's forehead.

Monty snarled a curse and tried to drag his sidearm from its holster, already knowing he wasn't going to make it. He thought of his wife holding their baby girl in his final second of life before the bullets tore into his skull.

Team Reaper Headquarters

Thurston got off the phone with Traynor and immediately called General Jones. He answered on the third ring and immediately said, "Be advised, Mary, I'm with the President."

"Perfect, put me on speaker."

A brief pause, then: "Go ahead, Mary. We can both hear you."

"Johnny Jihad is dead."

"Oh, thank God," President Carter said.

"One hundred percent confirmed?" Jones asked.

"Slick is sending you the photos right now." She snapped her fingers at the computer wizard, who nodded.

"Excellent."

"But there's another problem," Thurston said.

"What's that?"

"We think there's going to be an attack on One Police Plaza in New York City today."

"How sure are you?"

"Not one hundred percent, but pretty sure."

Jones got right down to business. "Tell me what you need."

"Can you scramble a chopper out of McGuire to pick up Reaper Five and Bravo Two at the marina?"

"You're thinking of neutralizing the threat from the air?"

"Unless you've got a better play."

"No, that's as good a plan as any. I'll send a couple of Apaches to give your boys a lift. If we can identify the target, or targets, we'll blow them to hell and back."

"We also need to evacuate One Police Plaza ASAP, and as much of the surrounding area as you can."

"I'll make the call as soon as we hang up."

"Then I won't keep you. Just one more thing."

"Name it."

"I need you to put Bravo Two in touch with the commanding officers of the Manhattan North and South Boroughs and tell them to follow his instructions."

"I'll make that happen as soon as the chopper picks him up."

"Copy that."

"Thurston?" President Carter said.

"Yes, sir?"

"Tell your team I said nice work."

"Thank you, sir. But we're not done yet."

———

New Jersey / New York

The rubberneckers whipped out their cell phones again when the two Apache gunships landed in the marina parking lot, whipping up clouds of dust like a Saudi Arabian sandstorm.

As soon as Traynor climbed into the Boeing AH-64's cockpit and settled into the gunner's chair, he put on the helmet and almost immediately heard the pilot's voice coming through the com. "I've been told your call-sign is Bravo Two and your buddy is Reaper Five. You can call me Deadshot. The other pilot goes by Gator, on account he's a Cajun boy. Welcome aboard."

"Thanks for the ride," Traynor said as he buckled up. "Why do they call you Deadshot?"

"Because whatever I shoot at gets dead," came the chuckled reply.

"With Hellfires and a chain gun, they damn well better," Traynor said. "You've been briefed on the mission?"

"Ten-four. Stop a terrorist attack on One Police Plaza. Just give me and Gator a target, and we'll take care of the rest."

"Working on it."

As they lifted off, Deadshot said, "Fifteen minutes to Manhattan. Meanwhile, I'm patching a call through to you."

"Copy that."

A moment later a new voice came through the com. "Bravo Two, this is Assistant Chief Steven O'Reilly, Commanding Office of the Manhattan South Patrol Borough. I've got Assistant Chief Jeffrey Hughes with me, from Manhattan North. Some very important people ordered us to get in touch with you and follow your instructions. What have you got for us?"

Traynor said, "Cutting right to the chase, gentlemen, One Police Plaza has been targeted for a terror strike."

"So we've been told. Evacuation procedures have been initiated."

"Good."

"Any idea what shape the attack will take?" Hughes asked.

"Affirmative," Traynor replied. "A car bomb. They used Semtex on the cruise ship and church, so we're guessing more of the same here."

"There's no way to just drive a car up to 1PP," O'Reilly said. "We planned for that when we built the place. There are barriers everywhere."

"Civilian vehicles, maybe," Traynor responded. "But what about police cars?"

The radio silence let him know he now had their full attention as the ramifications hit home.

"My God," O'Reilly finally said. "They could just drive right in, and we wouldn't bat an eye."

"What do you need from us, Bravo Two?" Hughes asked.

"The documents we seized from the terrorists indicated they planned on hijacking a police cruiser. Do you have a way to contact all your patrol units at the same time?"

"Affirmative."

"Send every squad car within a mile radius to some

emergency. Make one up, an all-hands-on-deck scenario. Tell them there's been another terrorist attack for all I care. Just get them going away from 1PP. The car that keeps rolling toward 1PP will be our bomber. We'll take them out from the air."

"Roger that," Hughes said. "We'll do it now."

"Wait ten minutes," Traynor replied. "We need to be in position when you make the call."

"Got it."

"Thanks, gentlemen. Bravo Two out."

As the Apaches soared through the air like steel dragons, powered to over 200 mph by their twin turboshafts, the New York City skyline appeared in the distance. Traynor briefly thought about Mike Reardon, laid up in a hospital bed. He wondered if Omega would even bother to return to finish the job now that the DEA-cartel alliance had been crushed. Hopefully the assassin would just fade into the shadows and never resurface, happy to have survived the Reaper blitz, and just leave Mike and Jeremy to live their lives in peace.

The pilot's voice interrupted his thoughts. "Deadshot to Bravo Two, you awake up there?"

"Just enjoying the scenery. Something on your mind?"

"Couldn't help but overhear your little chat. You say we're dealing with Semtex?"

"Not sure, but that's our best guess."

"That could be a problem," Deadshot said. "Because when we find that car, we're gonna shred it with the chainguns."

Traynor caught on immediately. "You're worried the Semtex will blow."

"We hit one of the detonators, and it's gonna be big-bang time."

"Chance we'll have to take," Traynor said. "They're gonna blow it up anyway, so we might as well take a shot at stopping them."

"Your call, Bravo Two. Just wanted to point out the risk."

Minutes later, they thundered across the Hudson River and entered the airspace over Manhattan. As they banked around the skyscrapers and peered down into the concrete canyons, they saw dozens of police cars, lights flashing, tearing down the city streets.

"There go the good guys," Traynor said, not happy about having to send the boys in blue on a wild goose chase, but knowing it was the right play. He doubted there was a cop down there that wouldn't understand once it was explained to them. "Now let's find our bad boys."

———

Brooklyn, New York

Paul and Rick stripped the police officer's uniforms off their bodies, then managed to stuff the corpses in the trunk. On a normal day, this would have been impossible to accomplish without witnesses, but the series of attacks had left the city streets a ghost town. Those that could flee to safer parts had done so; those that could not had hunkered down in their homes and apartments to ride out the storm of violence.

Inside the trunk, they found duffel bags containing various police-related supplies, including lightweight jackets with POLICE emblazoned across the back in reflective lettering. These served perfectly to conceal the suicide vests they wore, each bearing five pounds of Semtex. They would insert the detonators at the last minute. No point in risking an accidental detonation while they were rolling to the target.

Their plan was to drive right up to One Police Plaza and walk inside, using the officers' guns to shoot their way as far into the heart of the building as they could before detonating the explosives, killing scores of infidels, and earning their passage to paradise. If the rumors of virgins were true, so much the better. Once Paul and Rick got there, those virgins wouldn't remain virginal for long.

As they settled back into the police cruiser, they turned off the radio thirty seconds before a high priority call went out dispatching all units to an active shooter situation. They didn't want the distraction of radio chatter as they prayed their final prayers, begging Allah to honor their sacrifice and welcome them home.

Prayers completed and souls ready for their final mission, Paul put the cruiser in gear and merged onto the approach for the Brooklyn Bridge. There was almost no traffic on the bridge to impede their progress, but Paul hit the lights and siren anyway. With the siren's banshee wail for a soundtrack, they sped toward their date with martyrdom.

———

As the Apaches circled above the city like giant birds of prey, it was Brick who spotted the cruiser. "Reaper Five to all call signs, suspect spotted. Brooklyn Bridge."

Deadshot immediately banked his gunship toward the iconic landmark. Out his window, Traynor saw the police cruiser nearing the middle of the bridge, lights flashing.

The other Apache was closer. "Bravo Two to Gator, you need to stop that car."

"Roger that, Bravo Two."

The Apache reached the bridge in mere seconds. It swung around and dropped down to block the incoming police cruiser. Traynor knew the 30mm M230 chainguns were slaved to Gator and Deadshot's helmets using the Integrated Helmet and Display Sighting System, meaning the weapons would track the pilots' head movements and point wherever they looked. Traynor had no doubt Gator's M230 was aimed right at the squad car, which had screeched to a halt to avoid ramming nose-first into the assault chopper.

"Gator to Bravo Two, this is your party. Want me to light 'em up?"

"Negative, Gator. Not until we're sure those are the bogeys and not just some boys in blue taking the scenic route."

The police cruiser slammed into reverse, smoking the rear tires and leaving behind strips of rubber.

"Bravo Two to Deadshot, cut him off."

"Thought you might say that." Deadshot brought the Apache around and dropped into position behind the reversing cruiser.

"Give 'em a warning shot," Traynor ordered.

The M230 roared to life, spewing flame like dragon's breath. Asphalt exploded all around the cop car as the 30mm rounds tore into the road. The cruiser halted again.

"They tried to run." Deadshot's voice came through the com. "That proof enough?"

"Negative," Traynor replied. "I might hit reverse too if a fucking Apache showed up in front of me. We need more proof."

As if on cue, the cruiser's doors opened and two men wearing police jackets came out firing pistols. The jackets were unbuttoned to reveal the suicide vests beneath.

"That proof enough?" Deadshot asked.

"There's our dirtbags," Traynor growled. "Hit 'em!"

Both chainguns cut loose at the same time, sending 30mm bullets scorching downrange at a blistering rate of 300 rounds per minute. The two terrorists were obliterated beyond anything resembling human beings, shredded into crimson slurry by the chainguns, flesh and bone dissolving in the devastating crossfire. By the time the M230s stopped firing, the terrorists' remains were strewn all over the bridge. The coroner wouldn't need anything more than a shovel and a plastic bag.

"Deadshot to Bravo Two, the targets have been terminated."

Traynor was impressed by the firepower he had just witnessed. "Bravo Two to Deadshot... no shit." He made a mental note to beg Thurston to acquire an Apache for the Team Reaper arsenal. They could always help themselves to some confiscated cartel money to help pay the $200 million price tag. Hell, he would go to school himself to learn to fly the warbird.

"Deadshot to Bravo Two, you're still calling the shots. What's next?"

"Head back to base, Deadshot." Traynor looked out the cockpit window at what remained of the dead terrorists. The mission was over. "Time to go home."

CHAPTER 15

Angel of Mercy Hospital
Twenty-eight hours later

Traynor answered his phone on the second ring. "Hello?"

"We're here," Kane said. "Reardon awake?" He kept his voice flat, emotionless. He and Traynor still had some shit to sort out, but first things first.

"He's awake," Traynor replied. "Come on up."

"He knows the kid got a little banged up, right?"

"He knows."

"Okay. We're on our way."

Five minutes later, Jeremy Reardon rushed into the hospital room. His eyes lit up when he saw his father. "Daddy!" A big white bandage formed a puffy dome around the kid's right ear.

Kane and Cara stood in the doorway as Jeremy climbed onto the bed and snuggled into his father's arms. As reunions went, this was a good one. Tears spilled down Reardon's cheeks as he held his son as best he could limited by his crippled leg and assorted wounds.

Reardon finally pulled away enough to look at Kane. "Thank you," he said. "Thank you for giving me back my boy."

Kane nodded. "No thanks necessary. You helped us take down a nasty cartel enterprise, and you paid a hell of a price for it."

"The one who ordered..." He hesitated, glanced at Jeremy, then back at Kane. "You know..."

Kane nodded. "The man who gave the order took one right between the eyes."

Reardon nodded. "Thanks for that." He paused, then added, "I thought it would make me feel better, but it doesn't."

"Nothing will make it better but time," Kane replied. "Trust me, I know."

Reardon gave him a nod, then turned back to Jeremy.

Kane looked at Traynor. "I think it's time you and I had a chat, Pete."

He nodded. "Yeah, let's get this over with."

They grabbed a coffee at the cafeteria, then went outside to get some fresh air. The city had come back to life after President Carter announced yesterday evening that Johnny Jihad had been killed by "special forces" and that those same special forces, in conjunction with two unnamed—to prevent cartel retaliation—Apache pilots, had stopped another terrorist attack designed to decimate One Police Plaza. Overnight polls showed the President's approval rating had skyrocketed with the news.

They found a concrete bench around the corner and sat down. Neither man said anything, but the silence between them spoke volumes.

Traynor spoke first. "How's Carlos? Heard he took some lead in Colombia."

Kane nodded. "Some bandits caught us in an ambush. Arenas took two in the leg, one in the ribs. We got him fixed up last night and sent him off for some R and R with his family." Carlos' wife, daughter, and son had come to the United States when the ex-Mexican Special Forces operator joined Team Reaper.

Traynor sipped from his coffee. "That's good."

Kane sighed, then dumped the rest of his coffee on the ground—it tasted like lukewarm mud anyway, just like all hospital java—and crushed the paper cup in his fist. "No, Pete, it's not good. He took three bullets while you sat on your ass."

Traynor's head whipped around. "The hell is that crap, Reaper? Are you seriously blaming me for Carlos getting wounded?"

"Directly blaming you? No," Kane replied. "But the fact of the matter is, you weren't there, and you should have been."

"And just leave Mike to fend for himself? He was attacked, Reaper. Omega crippled him and slashed him to ribbons, but you expected me to just leave him lying in a hospital bed and fly off to the land of coffee and coke?"

"Yeah," Kane said. "That's exactly what I expected."

"Mike and I went through some bloody times together, Reaper. He's my brother, and I had to have his six."

Kane fixed him with a piercing stare. "Are you saying the members of Team Reaper aren't your brothers?"

"Don't put words in my mouth. That's not what I said, and you know it."

"Kind of sounds like you did."

"Kiss my ass, Reaper. Of course, they're my brothers. I'd give my life for any of them."

"And yet you didn't have their six this time, and Carlos ended up down for the count."

"That's so un-fucking-fair that I can't even believe you would—"

Kane cut him off. "I know it's not your fault Carlos got hit."

"Sure as hell doesn't sound like it."

"Seriously, I do," Kane said. "But if you had been there if you'd had his six like you're supposed to, then maybe you could have stopped it from happening. Maybe one more gun would have made all the difference. I expect—no, *demand*—that everyone on this team never gives each other a reason to question their loyalty. But you chose your buddy over your teammates, and that raises a big question about where your loyalties lie."

Traynor drained his coffee and mimicked Kane by crushing the paper cup in his fist. Kane could see the veins in his tattooed arms bulging and knew the ex-DEA agent was getting angry. Kane didn't care. Saying the hard words was part of being a leader.

Traynor rose from the bench, walked stiff-legged over to a trash receptacle, and threw away the crumpled cup. When he came back, he towered over Kane, who remained seated. "That's some real crap you're spouting, Reaper," he said. "The kind of crap that some might say deserves a punch in the mouth."

Now Kane stood up. He did it slowly, calmly, sure of himself. Traynor was tall, but Kane was taller. He took a step back, arms hanging loosely at his side. "Go ahead and get it done then," Kane said. "First shot's free. The rest you'll have to earn."

Traynor bunched up his fists. Tension burned hot between the two warriors and for a few strained moments,

Kane thought Traynor would actually take a swing. But then the anger seemed to abruptly drain out of him like air from a punctured balloon. "I'm not going to hit you, Reaper," he said, slumping back down onto the bench. "Just kick me off the team and get it over with."

Kane remained standing. "That what you want?"

"Doesn't much matter what I want, does it?"

"I'm asking."

"Why?"

"Because I want to hear the answer."

Traynor leaned back, rubbing his hands over his bearded face. "If you're asking me if I want to get kicked off the team, then the answer is no."

"But do you understand my position?"

"Yeah," Traynor said begrudgingly. "Yeah, I guess I see where you're coming from. But it was an impossible choice to make, Reaper. Loyalty to my brother from the old days, or loyalty to my brothers in the here and now." He gave Kane a look that was both regretful and tinged with defiance. "It wasn't like I didn't want to be there in Colombia with you guys. I just felt Mike needed me more and I couldn't walk away."

Kane looked him dead in the eye. "And that's why I'm not telling you to pack up and get off my team."

Traynor clearly wasn't expecting that. "You're not?"

"No. Like I said, I demand my team shows loyalty to their brothers. You did that. You stood watch over a fallen brother. That kind of loyalty, that kind of brotherhood, is exactly what I want on Team Reaper."

Traynor stood up again and faced him, features solemn. "I appreciate that, Reaper. I really do. I hope to God I never have to make that kind of choice again."

"You and me both," Kane reached out and clapped

Traynor on the shoulder. "Consider yourself on a leave of absence. Stick around here until Reardon is ready to take care of himself. We'll hold things down until you're back."

"Thanks. But if something pops, give me a call. You have my word I'll be there."

"With a pistol in each hand, right?"

"And a knife between my teeth." Traynor grinned.

Cara rounded the corner. "There you boys are." Her eyes flicked back and forth between the two men, figuring out where things stood. "All good?"

"Yeah," Traynor said. "He tried to fire me, but I told him I wasn't going."

"How'd that work out?" Cara asked.

"We thumb-wrestled for it," Traynor replied. "Reaper lost."

"Yeah," Kane snorted. "That's how it all went down."

Cara smiled. "Glad it all worked out." She looked at Kane. "Reaper, I'm starving. Let's go find a steak before we head back to HQ."

"Sounds like a plan to me."

"Great. I'm just going to use the ladies room. I'll meet you at the Jeep."

Both men watched her walk away. Sure, she was a fellow warrior, but she was also a woman, and their eyes looked where men's eyes are prone to look.

"So is it true she's got a picture of Donald Duck tattooed where the sun don't shine?" Traynor asked.

Kane smiled and shook his head. "A gentleman never tells, right?"

"You're a lucky man, Reaper."

"Was," he corrected, with just a hint of regret in his voice. "Not anymore."

Traynor snorted. "Yeah, okay, you two keep acting like

it's over. The rest of us are smart enough to know that things are just on pause."

Kane gave him a crooked grin. "Time will tell, I guess."

They said their goodbyes and Kane made his way to the parking garage next to the hospital. Cara might be craving a ribeye, but with the mission now behind them, Kane was thinking it was time for a celebratory shot of whiskey. Maybe even two shots.

Visiting hours were almost over, so the parking garage was only half-full. Kane's hand was reaching for the door handle of the Jeep when a scruffy cat bolted from beneath the vehicle and raced away with a yowling screech. A second later it went sprawling in a boneless tumble as its head vanished in a red smudge.

Kane recognized the sound of a suppressed gunshot and spun around, drawing his Sig M17. But the stranger already had him dead to rights; the suppressor-equipped HK45 tactical pistol pointed at his chest. The gun gleamed black and ugly in the murky lights of the garage.

Kane kept the Sig down by his side, waiting to see how this would play out.

"I hate cats. Worthless animals," the gunman said. "Now, I see you managed to pull your piece. Do me a favor and drop it."

"I'd rather not."

"It wasn't a request. Besides, you've got nothing to worry about... for now. I'm not here to kill you unless you make me. I just want to talk."

"Not much for chit-chat," Kane replied.

The stranger smiled, and it was a mirthless smile. He was tall, almost as tall as Kane, with buzzed hair and flat eyes that had seen things that deadened a man's soul. Whoever this guy was, he had danced with the devil a time or two. Kane had no doubt there was blood on the man's hands, and he had a strong suspicion whose blood it was.

"Drop your weapon," the gunman said. "I won't ask you again."

Kane shrugged. "Man with the gun makes the rules." He let the Sig fall to the concrete. He still had a Ka-Bar sheathed under his jacket and began calculating how to close the ten-meter gap between them so he could bring the blade into the game. "So, what do you want to talk about?"

"Let's talk about your team, Reaper, and how I'm going to kill every last one of them after I finish the job on Reardon."

So, you're Omega, Kane thought. *Nice to meet you, asshole.* He didn't try to play dumb. The guy clearly had sensitive information and wasting time acting stupid wasn't going to get him anywhere. "How the hell do you know about my team?" he asked.

Omega smiled thinly. "You're a drug task force with ties to the DEA. I also happen to have a connection with the DEA and a high enough security clearance to dig up the dirt on you and your merry band of mutts."

"Did you dig deep enough to figure out we're not people you want to fuck with?"

Omega's grin widened. "Yeah, yeah. Always fear the Reaper, right?"

Kane shrugged. "You said it, not me."

"What if I said I wanted to join your team?"

"I'd tell you we don't hire psychopaths."

"That's rich, coming from you," Omega countered. "Sure, I've killed people. But you and your team killed more people in the last seventy-two hours than I've killed in my entire life. But yeah, sure, I'm the brain-twisted psycho."

Kane had no regrets about who he had killed. He eyed

the gun trained on him and felt the numbers running down toward zero as he rasped, "They had it coming."

"We all got it coming."

A hospital security guard chose that unfortunate moment to step out of the elevator. He was young and unarmed, but Kane seriously doubted that mattered to a heartless killer like Omega.

The guard saw the gun pointed at Kane, and his eyes nearly bugged out of his head. "Hey!" he shouted, pointing at the assassin. "Put it down!" He reached for the nightstick at his side. Even with the gravity of the moment, Kane couldn't help but think there was a tragic joke in there about bringing a club to a gunfight.

But it was no laughing matter when Omega, in the blink of an eye, swung his pistol around and pumped two bullets into the guard's chest, drilling right through the tin badge he wore over his heart. The guard catapulted backward as blood splashed all over the elevator doors.

While the man's casual murder infuriated Kane, he nevertheless seized the opening the fickle gods of war had given him. He launched himself forward as Omega started to bring the pistol back into play. He closed the gap faster than the assassin had anticipated, slamming into him a split second before he fired. The impact caused the shot to go wide and smack into the door of a nearby Lexus. The shrieking noise of a car alarm filled the parking garage like the soundtrack to the apocalypse.

As they crashed to the ground, Kane managed to knock the gun from Omega's hand. He also managed to draw his Ka-Bar, but before he could even think about using it, Omega drove a knee into his groin and used the leverage to flip him over his head. Kane felt himself airborne for a moment, then hit the ground hard, with a loud thud like a slab of beef dropped on the butcher's table. His mashed balls screamed for payback, demanding that he ram the knife between Omega's ribs and carve his name into the assassin's black, beating heart.

He quickly powered to his feet. Omega did the same, and the two warriors faced each other. With a twisted smile, Omega drew a knife of his own, a Spyderco.

"You see this knife?" Omega taunted. "I'm gonna stick it in you."

"I'm guessing you're not a big believer in 'no means no.'" Kane held the Ka-Bar low, ready to move in for a disemboweling strike.

"You know, Reaper, I think I'm done talking," Omega said. "I think it's time to kill you."

"About damn time," Kane growled. "I thought you'd never shut up."

"Let's dance."

They met in a clash of razored steel and thudding fists. Kane sucked in his gut as Omega's blade sliced through his shirt and kissed the skin beneath. He responded with a vicious left cross that caught Omega's jaw, snapping his head to the side. But when he tried to seize the opening and thrust the Ka-Bar up under his enemy's chin, Omega managed to evade the blow.

Kane pushed his attack, stabbing low, going for the belly. But Omega quickly sidestepped, and Kane missed. The Spyderco flicked out and cut a gash in his left shoulder as punishment for his failure.

Kane ignored the pain and dropped into a crouch, spinning toward his opponent at the same time. He slashed with the knife, aiming the ankle tendon. But once again, Omega dodged the strike, and instead of cutting flesh, Kane's knife scraped concrete.

"Nice try," Omega said. "But if those are your best moves, then you're gonna die."

"Thought you said you were done running your mouth," Kane rasped. He had to find a way to take Omega out, but he was starting to suspect the assassin was simply better with a blade and was just toying with him.

As if to prove the point, Omega suddenly lunged at him. Kane retreated, but Omega was too fast. In a blur of motion, the killer came in low and without even knowing how it happened, Kane found the Spyderco stuck in the meat of his thigh.

Omega reached down with his other hand and grabbed Kane's ankle, throwing him off balance. Kane went down on his back, hot pain burning through his stab wound, with Omega riding his chest.

Omega left the knife buried in Kane's leg and wrapped vice-like fingers around his neck. Kane snarled like a wild animal that knows it's about to die and tried to knock the hands away, but they were relentless steel bands that constricted mercilessly. Omega's thumbs dug into his throat, pressing on his windpipe, cutting off his oxygen. Black stars exploded across his vision. He fought to stay conscious, his survival instinct simply refusing to tap out. He knew he was seconds away from terminal blackout.

"Game over, Reaper," Omega said. "Don't fight it, just let it happen. That's what I'm going to tell your bitch Cara too, right while I'm fucking her to death."

He heard her voice then, distant and muffled like he was underwater.

"Fuck *this*, asshole," Cara snarled, ramming her Sig against the back of his neck and pulling the trigger.

The bullet ripped apart Omega's throat and exited through his face, blowing off half his lower jaw. Kane felt the spatter of hot blood, then sucked in a deep breath as Omega's fingers relinquished their hold on his throat.

Before the first shot had even finished echoing off the concrete walls, Cara followed up with a strategically-placed kill-shot, putting a round right above Omega's ear. The assassin's skull came apart like a hammered egg.

Kane pushed the corpse off him and looked at Cara as she stood a few yards away, smoke curling from the muzzle of her gun. He coughed and hacked, trying to ease the pain of his throttled throat. He reached down and pulled the knife out of his thigh with a grimace.

Cara holstered her Sig. "Can't leave you alone for five minutes, Reaper."

Kane climbed to his feet. "Tell me about it." His voice sounded raspy, just a notch or two above a barely intelligible growl. Still, he was alive. His voice might be shot for a few days, but it was better than being dead. "Thanks for saving my ass."

She smiled, with a bit of a wicked glint. "Well, I am kind of fond of that ass."

"I owe you one."

Her smile widened and the wickedness increased. "Well, I know just how you can pay me back."

"Cara, we've talked about this..."

"And maybe it's time to stop talking if you know what I mean." She gestured toward the blood-splattered corpse. "Who was that guy, anyway?"

Kane retrieved his gun and slid it back into the holster. "Omega."

"The hitter who almost killed Reardon? That Omega?"

"That's him."

"Glad I smoked him."

"You and me both." Sirens howled in the distance. Cops summoned by the gunshots. "We need to get out of here."

"I'll drive," Cara said. "You look like you just got the crap kicked out of you."

"That would be an accurate assessment."

"Never thought I'd see the day Reaper got his butt whipped."

"It happens to all of us eventually."

As they climbed into the Jeep, Cara asked, "Where to?"

Strapping on his seatbelt, Kane suddenly felt a weariness wash over him. He wanted, perhaps even needed, a respite, however brief, from the violence and savagery. He wasn't sure it would be wise to take things all the way again with Cara, but he couldn't think of a better person to share some downtime with. "Let's find some dinner. I could use a cold beer right about now."

"Looks to me like you could use something a little stronger than beer."

"Yeah, well." Kane grinned. "Whiskey works too."

Cara said, "You know you're bleeding, right?"

"So find a place that doesn't mind a little blood."

They drove off into the night. As they hit the city streets, Kane knew tomorrow might bring more blood and death to further scar their warrior souls, but for right now, the mission was over. They couldn't rest—never that—but they could at least let their guns cool.

Until they had to take them out again.

Because that's just the way it was.

Death was their life.

A LOOK AT: RELENTLESS

A TEAM REAPER THRILLER

It's their most brutal assignment yet.

After a mission in Somalia sees them rescued by an Australian SAS team, Reaper and his people return to the U.S. where a raid on a warehouse sets into motion a chain of events which will lead them on a violent search for one of their own.

The team hits Europe with the force of a runaway train, gathering intel which leads them to Pripyat in the Ukraine and an auction like they've never encountered before. Then to Italy and a conspiracy which, if carried out, will rock the religious world to its core.

It's up to Team Reaper to stop it, down two team members, and with no idea who is behind it.

AVAILABLE JUNE 2019 FROM BRENT TOWNS AND WOLFPACK PUBLISHING

ABOUT THE AUTHOR

Mark Allen was raised by an ancient clan of ruthless ninjas and now that he has revealed this dark secret, he will most likely be dead by tomorrow for breaking the sacred oath of silence. The ninjas take this stuff very seriously.

When not practicing his shuriken-throwing techniques or browsing flea markets for a new katana, Mark writes action fiction. He prefers his pose to pack a punch, likes his heroes to sport twin Micro-Uzis a la Chuck Norris in Invasion USA, and firmly believes there is no such thing as too many headshots in a novel.

He started writing "guns 'n' guts" (his term for the action genre) at the not-so-tender age of 16 and soon won his first regional short story contest. His debut action novel, The Assassin's Prayer, was optioned by Showtime for a direct-to-cable movie. When that didn't pan out, he published the book on Amazon to great success, moving over 10,000 copies in its first year, thanks to its visceral combination of raw, redemptive drama mixed with unflinching violence.

Now, as part of the Wolfpack team, Mark Allen looks forward to bringing his bloody brand of gun-slinging, bullet-blasting mayhem to the action-reading masses.

Mark currently resides in the Adirondack Mountains of upstate New York with a wife who doubts his ninja skills because he's always slicing his fingers while chopping veggies, two daughters who refuse to take tae kwon do, let alone ninjitsu, and enough firepower to ensure that he is never bothered by door-to-door salesmen.

https://wolfpackpublishing.com/mark-allen/

Look for the Next *Team Reaper* Novel Coming Soon!

Made in the USA
Las Vegas, NV
15 February 2023

67550549R00142